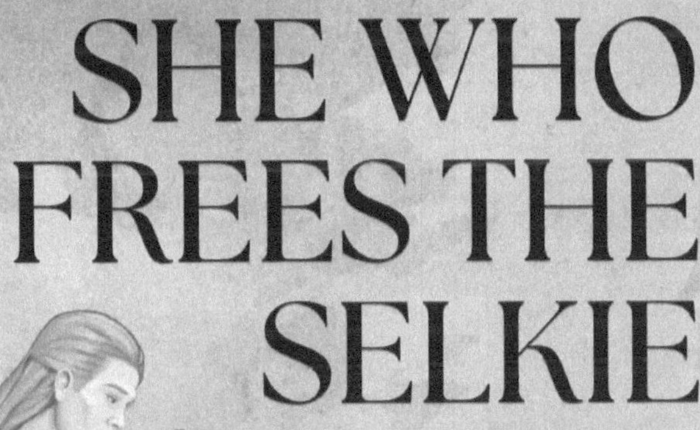

SHE WHO FREES THE SELKIE

K. MALADY

Also By

THE ASCEND TRIALS
YA fantasy romance adventure

THE HARMONY CHRONICLES
NA paranormal romance/contemporary fantasy

THREADS OF FATE
NA/Adult romantic fantasy retellings

KNEELING KINGDOMS
Adult interconnected standalone romantasy

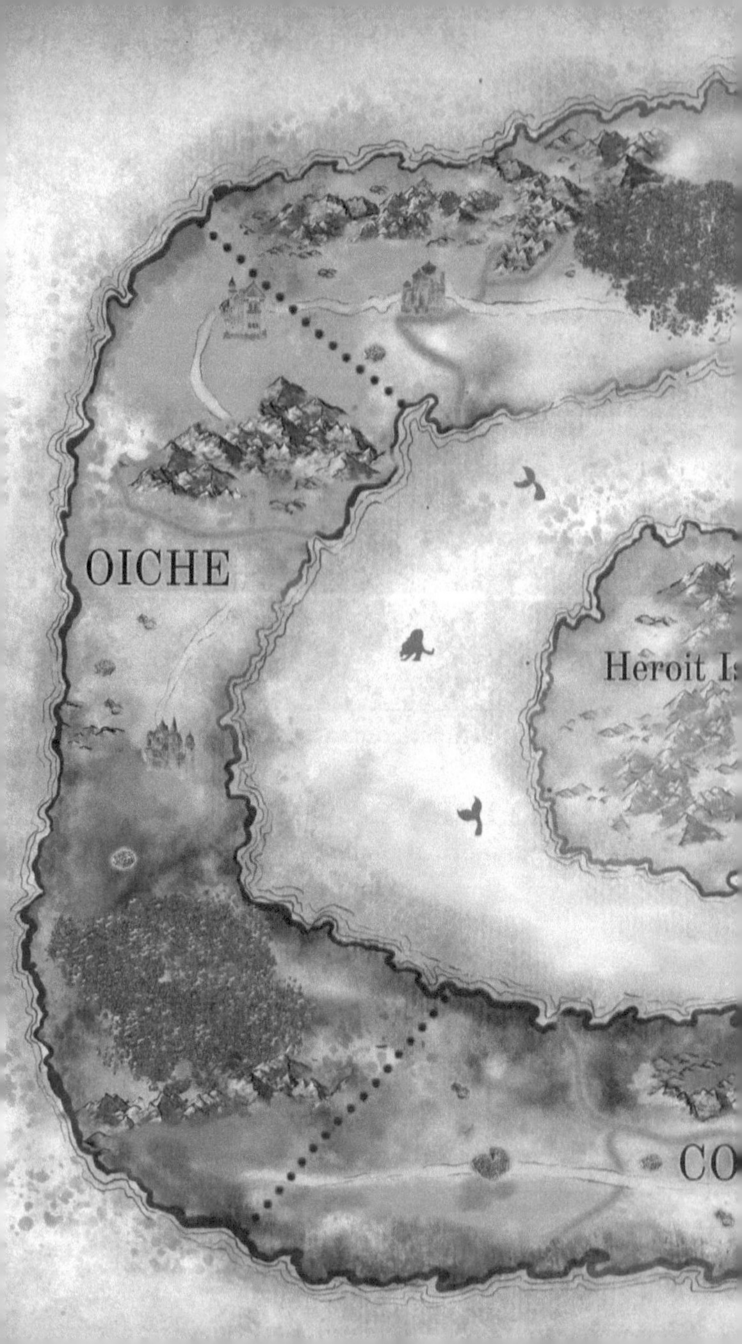

OICHE
Heroit I
CO

A
The
Aboveground
EALACH
Prism Lake
A
J

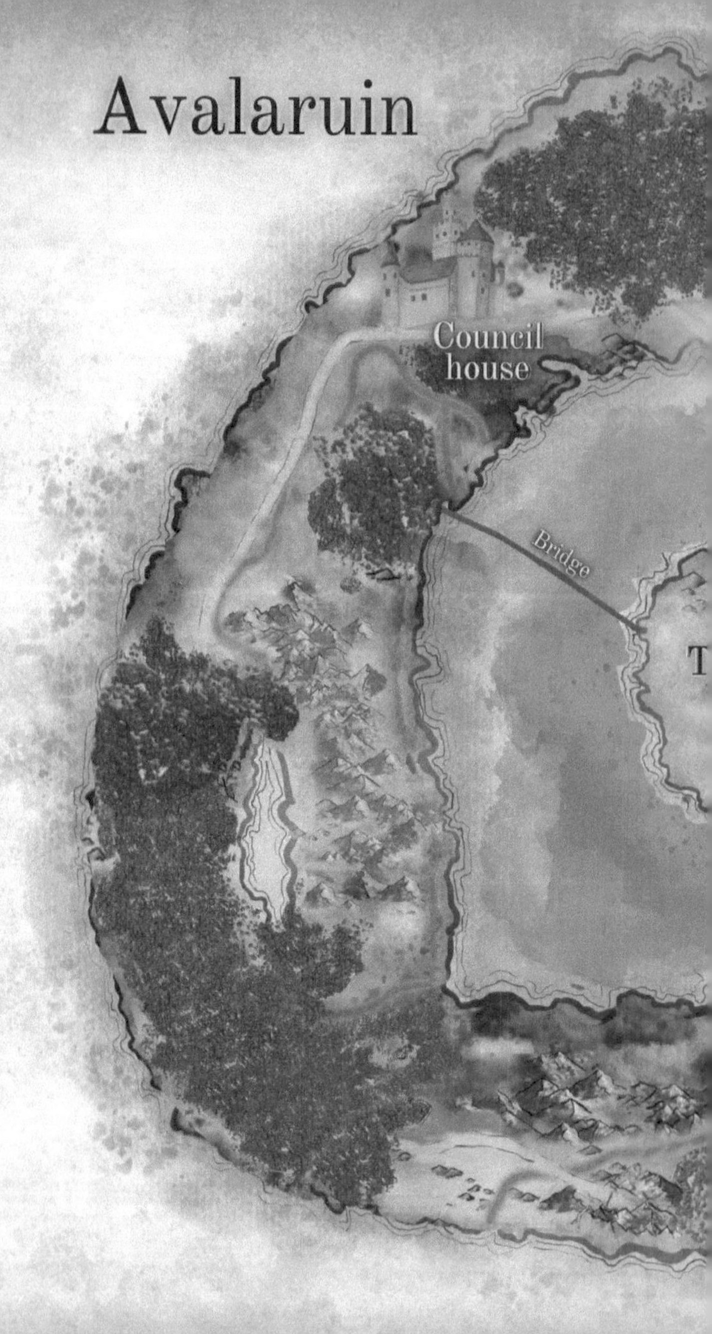

Avalaruin
Council house
Bridge
T

Castle
Bridge
and
Unseen Lake

Chapter 1

As a resident of Latha, a purely human settlement, it is easy to become complacent and unaware of the vast world beyond. But it is crucial to remain informed of the broader realm that lies beyond our borders. Millennia ago, under the reign of the High King Diarmaid, the fae used their profound magic to create a new realm parallel to their own, known as the Aboveground. This world *became home to various beings, including humans, werewolves, vampires, and non-fae human magic practitioners now known as 'mages.' Meanwhile, the fae and their lesser kin remain in Avalaruin, a world considered upside-down of our own. However, the boundaries between these realms are not impenetrable. Certain creatures, such as shape shifting beings found in the waters near the portal, traverse both worlds, bridging the divide between the Above-ground and Avalaruin. Understanding these interactions is essential to grasp the full scope of our interconnected existence.*

-Excerpt from Beneath the Surface: Unveiling the Mysteries of Selkies and Finfolk.

It's nearly dusk as I sit on the weathered rocks by the shore, knees drawn tight against my chest while I watch the waves crash against the jagged edges. The sound of the water is a constant refrain for my life—the sharp roar during storms, the gentle caress when the wind is still, the frothy spray during high tides. In the distance are the fishing boats, their sails billowing like ghosts against the twilight sky. Soon, they'll return and my evening chores will begin.

My callused fingers graze the gritty pebbles and shells beneath me. As a child, I loved the sound of the sea. I'd sit in Mama's lap and watch the water from the northern shore. I wasn't allowed in the water—too dangerous—but Mama never got in either.

With her amber-brown eyes alight—ones with irises that swirl like a whirlpool, ones I inherited—she'd make up stories about the seaweed and driftwood that littered the beach, turning insignificant objects tossed about by the sea into magical treasures. And she'd tell me tales of the wonders found in the deep. The grindylows in the ponds, the kelpies in the marshes, the sirens in the sea, and the selkies in the shallows. The selkies were her favorite and made appearances in nearly every tale. Those stories became my earliest books. I'd thought they were fiction at first, jokes to tell children. Certainly vampires exist, but aquatic shapeshifters?

Mama finally convinced me, though not how she probably expected. Because one of those shapeshifters took her.

At least Mama loved the water. I think if she had fins, she would have willingly lived within it. I don't know if that makes it better or worse. Since then, books have been my only refuge, my escape into worlds far beyond this shore.

I pull my scraggly shawl tighter around my broad shoulders, trying to ward off the chill. A tinge of salt lingers in the air, coating the inside of my mouth and leaving a bitter aftertaste.

I stand and turn back inland, where the thatched roofs of our village cottages and shacks cluster together, huddled against the relentless sea. Our own cottage lopes to the side, with chipped paint Dad hadn't fixed since... since Mama disappeared.

It's funny, though, how it happened.

We live on the distant northern shore of the land, so north that there are only a few streams and rivers that connect to Prism Lake, the crystal-clear water at the center of the Aboveground, home to the sirens. Surrounding the Lake are the human, vampire, mage, and werewolf settlements. Sure, some creatures—like selkies—straddle the borderline of the water, but the rest live in Avalaruin, an upside-down world beneath ours ruled by the fae. Go deep enough in the water on our side of the world and you end up in the upside-down where Prism Lake turns into the Unseen Lake, a dark abyss full of monstrous beings like the finfolk. The finfolk are shapeshifters, turning from grotesque fish into slightly amphibious humans. They roam the water, swimming up into Prism Lake and searching the nearby shores for human captives to enslave.

Mama was stolen by the finfolk—a finborn man, in fact—twenty years ago. Which means that a finborn had to come up from the deep, travel *miles* up shore to the northernmost settlement of the world, capture Mama, and return to Avalaruin. As a child, I thought it sounded unreal. As an adult, I've learned that some creatures will go through hell if they can hurt another on their way.

A crack of lightning streaks across the sky, followed by a deafening rumble of thunder, pulling me from my sour thoughts.

The fishing ship will be returning soon; I need to prepare for their arrival. Once I yank open the cracked wooden door to the cottage and make it inside, I switch out my damp shawl for an apron. My amber hair is a wild mess, untamed by the sea breeze and bleached at the ends from the sun, and

I twist the wavy strands into a knot. The storm grows wilder, shaking the windows that look out to the sea. I quickly batten them down and start a fire in the ashy hearth where my bed pallet is.

Mama vanished on a night like this, a night where the sea raged against the shore with a violent fury. Dad had been out with the other fishers, battling against the elements to bring home what little bounty they could find. I was barely five years old then, but I remember the look in Mama's eyes as she stood by the window, her gaze fixed on the churning waves.

That night, after I'd fallen asleep on my mat by the fire, a finborn broke in. The sound of the storm must have covered the struggle, as it never woke me. The next morning, Dad and I discovered the wreckage of our cottage, things tossed and scattered everywhere. It looked as though the storm had found its way within. Even Dad's special trunk, something he kept locked with the key worn on a ribbon around his neck, was bashed into pieces.

"Girl!" The gruff call of Uncle Lorcan breaks through my thoughts, louder than the roaring winds. His voice always sounds raspy, a result of years of shouting over the howling winds and crashing waves. He and Dad will be hauling their catch into the gutting shack soon. I'll need to spend the next several hours cleaning the catch before it spoils.

But I don't traipse outside in the storm just yet, instead letting the fire warm me through. My single rebellion is refusing to come at his first call. If he'd used my name—Maeve—I *might* have listened. But Uncle Lorcan forgets I have an identity beyond being a tool for their needs. I will take my freedom where I can get it.

"Maeve, move your shit!" That's Dad's stern echo, clearer than Uncle's, but no kinder.

Reluctance coils within me, but I have no excuse to avoid them now, not now that Dad is involved. My feet move with routine resignation, carrying me towards the shack. The dilapidated structure looms in front of me, its walls worn and splintered, the roof sagging under the weight of years of neglect. Even through the torrential rain hitting my skin like needles, I can still smell the pungent scent of fish guts and blood. Every night I must spend within it just adds another bit of frustration to my miles' long tally.

"Isn't it enough that I spend my days mending the nets and salting the catch?" My words rise like bubbles, defiant yet doomed to burst upon reaching the surface. I muttered them to myself, but somehow Dad still heard.

"We all do our part," he says, his grizzled salt-and-pepper beard not hiding the sharp set of his jaw. It's like looking at a stranger when I see him, the only resemblance is that we're both short and squat. I got everything else from Mama, including the freckles that dot my tan nose and cheeks in the sun.

"Go before I get angry," Dad adds, his blue eyes icy, giving me a hard slap on the back to shunt me inside.

Uncle Lorcan stands beside the net they've dragged from the boat, pooling water and blood onto the grimy wooden floor. One boot, caked with salt and seaweed, rests on top of the spoils. One side of the net has been torn open, and I make a mental note to add 'darning it' to my list of tasks for tomorrow. Fish lay gasping amidst tangled seaweed inside it, silver scales glinting under the gas lamp above. The librarian says some human settlements have a newish invention called *electricity*, but no one here has the coin for such a privilege.

Uncle Lorcan flicks open a penknife to cut through the net, but I stop him and gently untie each knot and tangle instead. Once the pile is freed, I begin my nightly task. The sharp edge of my knife slices through the scales and flesh with practiced precision. The metallic tang of blood mingles with the briny scent of the sea, a reminder that all survival comes at a cost.

As my hands work, my mind wanders back to the sea, drifting like flotsam on the tide. I think of my mother and her love for it. *Did she ever truly enjoy this life? Did she find pleasure in all the hardship we endure just to bring in another measly catch?* Sometimes I wonder if she saw this world as I do now—a constant struggle for freedom and despair, intertwined like the seaweed in our nets. With the finfolk, is she at least happy in the water?

"Girl." My uncle's voice breaks through the haze of my thoughts, drawing me back to the present. "We caught something special today."

Despite the unwelcome nickname, my curiosity gets the best of me and I meet his brown-eyed gaze. His weathered face, etched with deep wrinkles from years of exposure to the elements, holds a glimmer of maniacal glee as he drags in a wriggling bundle. Intrigued, I wipe my blood-stained hands on my apron and approach where he stands just inside the doors.

He kicks at the bundle, causing it to shift and reveal a human-like figure wrapped in cloth. My heart skips a beat as I trace the outline of something—or *someone*—bound in ropes. With gnarled fingers, Dad unfurls the tarp covering the rest of the 'catch.'

It's a man, but only in the loosest definition. He's human-shaped with pale skin that has an otherworldly sheen resembling the ripple of scales catching the faint light. His white—not blond, but true white—hair is a tangled mess from the storm, sticking to his face and lean shoulders. And his irises... they're a startling shade of shifting gray, a silver maelstrom. But it's the scalelike sheen on his skin that tells me he's something alien. (After all, if 'strange swirling eyes' was a clue to someone being a shapeshifter, I'd be tied up beside him.)

"What *is* it?" I ask breathlessly, my voice steady despite the unease crawling beneath my skin.

"Caught ourselves a finborn, girl," Uncle Lorcan grunts, his face twisted in triumph as much as disgust.

As I shift closer, the creature glares at me, his features sharp as broken glass, cutting through the air with a snarl. He'd be handsome but for the menacing expression. The smell of rain mixed with the scent of sea salt clings to him, as if he just emerged from the ocean, more pleasant than the stench of our shack. A low growl rumbles in his throat when I pull the stained kerchief from his mouth, revealing sharp teeth that drip with blood. *Uncle Lorcan's handiwork, or Dad's? Could go either way.* His skin, where my fingers accidentally grazed against it, is cool and smooth to the touch, like a fish's scales.

"I'm not what you think," he hisses through clenched teeth, his face a rictus of pain. "I am a selkie, cursed to this monstrous form without my pelt."

The claim hangs heavy in the salty air, laden with an earnestness never heard in this room.

"*Could* he be a selkie?" I say, more to myself than my family.

Finfolk have come this far north before, we know that because of Mama, but why would a selkie? Selkies have more to fear from us than vice versa. Humans get ahold of selkie pelts, and they can practically control them. The stories say there are men who would force selkie women into being their brides, hiding their pelts away so they couldn't return to the water. They'd stay human until they stole their pelts back.

Selkies are otherwise similar to humans. *Finborn* look like monsters, if I remember right. When Mama disappeared, I found the only book on shapeshifters our small library had, something called *Beneath the Surface*, or the like. I'd only gotten through the first few chapters when Dad burned it in the fire. My visits to the library needed to be secret after that, but no other books on finfolk ever reappeared on the shelves.

But if he *is* a selkie, something Mama loved so dearly, I can't bring myself to let him suffer in our care like any other fish.

"Girl, don't be foolish," Uncle Lorcan growls, shoving me back until my hip slams against the wooden table. "You know better than to trust a finborn's lies," he reminds me sternly, his eyes flickering towards Dad for support.

The creature's gaze also reaches towards Dad, perhaps hoping to find an ally in him. He'll need to keep looking, as he has no allies here. "I mean no harm," the being insists, each word threaded with desperation. "If you release me, I will trouble you no longer."

Dad's broad-shouldered frame hunches over to scowl down at the creature. "I release you and let you return and tell everyone about Marta? No fuckin' way."

My brows furrow. Marta is Mama's name. *Tell everyone about... what? That Mama was taken by an enemy of their own species? Or does that mean he is a finborn?*

"Into the cage with him," Dad says.

He and Uncle Lorcan heave him into a rusted cage meant for drying fish, not imprisoning creatures of the deep. They maneuver the cage outside the doors, forcing him back into the storm.

"Finish up," Uncle adds, and they both shuffle into the house, leaving me alone with the storm and the creature.

I linger by the cage, watching as the creature's eyes dim with resignation. The wind howls around us, whipping my hair into a frenzy of dark strands. Rain pelts down, soaking through the layers of my clothes, but I hardly notice the cold seeping into my bones. *Is he a selkie or a finborn? Is he to be feared or pitied?*

"Please, you must believe me," the creature begs again. His eyes are filled with desperation and flicker towards mine in search of mercy. "If I do not find my pelt before the next full moon, I will be trapped in this form forever."

The storm rages on, thrashing against the wooden walls of the gutting shack beside us, its fury echoing the turmoil in my mind. I can barely see the creature in the rain. The full moon—the hunter's moon it's called this time of year—is barely more than a week away.

Could it be true? Is he a selkie cursed to roam the land without his pelt, condemned to a fate far worse than death? Or was this an elaborate ruse, a guise to deceive us into setting him free only for him to wreak havoc upon our village and steal more of our people?

A gust of wind tears through the air, sending a spray of icy rain across my face. I blink, the sting of it burning my eyes.

"Release me, and I'll grant whatever you desire," the creature promises, pressing against the iron bars that cage his lean form.

And that settles it. I've seen enough deceit in my brief life to recognize it, especially when it wears the face of desperation.

Stepping closer to the cage, I crouch down to his eye level. "What's your name?"

The corner of his mouth curls into a grin. "Silas," he offers. Raindrops trail down his skin, making his scalelike appearance glisten.

"Well, Silas," I say sharply. "You should figure out what I actually want before attempting to bribe me with false promises."

"There are no false promises," he says. He glowers at me, but I can see the shimmer of uncertainty in his eyes, perhaps realizing that his tactics of persuasion may not be as effective on someone like me.

I scoff, unable to suppress the bitter laugh that rises in my throat. "Keep telling yourself that." And with that, I return to the shack, burying any curiosity or sympathy towards him under layers of duty and resentment.

Chapter 2

One such creature is the finfolk, renowned for their shape shifting abilities, moving effortlessly between their aquatic form and that of a human. Those who do not reside near bodies of water often know little else about them, to their detriment. It is the finfolk's ability to blend into human society that gives them the power to lure unsuspecting humans into their underwater domain.

> -Excerpt from Beneath the Surface: Unveiling the Mysteries of Selkies and Finfolk.

The first day I avoid him, darning my nets inside the house, watching him through the window. He barely moves in the cage.

Even though he has plenty of room to stretch out his limbs, he stays seated at the center. I didn't notice last night how exposed he was, his fish-belly pale skin glistening in the sunlight that filters through the cage's rusted bars. His skin looks as if it has been dusted with starlight, glimmering and ethereal. Every now and again, he tilts his towards the sun, displaying the long pale line of his neck. And then those shifting eyes would snap to the window, as if he knew I was watching. I'd jump back, though being seen by him wouldn't be nearly as bad as Dad discovering my interest.

No matter the punishment I'll receive if I'm caught, I'm fascinated by him: a being from the water, with powers beyond my comprehension. Selkie or finborn, he's been out there, seen things, gone into those depths that give me hives thinking about. And yet, here he is, captured and confined in a cage like an exotic pet. A selkie without his pelt.

"He could be lying," I mutter to myself. "A trick, just like the finfolk used to take Mama." My heart clenches at the memory.

But if he's not lying... If he really is a selkie, trapped and desperate, waiting for someone to help him...

I shake my head sharply. What does it matter if he's a selkie? I let him leave and end up with nothing but trouble. The only way he'll ever see his pelt is if he found one for me too, so I could finally leave this place.

Pity it doesn't work that way.

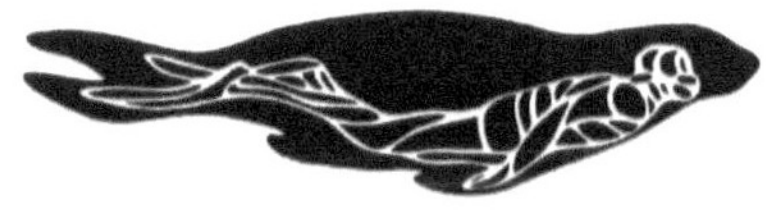

When night falls, I'm back in the gutting shack. My fingers deftly slice through the fish, but my mind lingers on Silas, visible through the open doors. His eyes are closed now, his face a mask of exhaustion and resignation.

A selkie. If he is telling the truth, then he's one of the creatures my mother loved, the ones from her stories. And yet, he sits there bound and caged, the same as a fish caught in one of our nets.

Dad and Uncle Lorcan are bickering about today's catch, something about finding a new spot, when I venture a question.

"What are we going to do with the creature?" I ask. My voice trembles slightly, betraying my nerves.

Dad's sneer is quick and sharp as he glances towards the cage outside, his eyes narrowing in contempt. "We'll wait for him to shift back into a finborn," he replies, his tone dismissive.

"And if he doesn't shift?" I press.

"Then he stays in the cage," Dad says firmly, leaving no room for discussion.

But something inside me pushes forward, like the heroines in my books, challenging the unspoken rules of our household. "He says he's a selkie."

Dad's gaze meets mine, cold and unwavering. "He's not."

"How can you be so sure?" My voice wavers again, betraying the courage I'm trying to muster.

Dad's face darkens as he stomps across the room to loom over me. The gaslamp casts sharp shadows across him, making him appear more ominous than the finfolk from my nightmares. "Shut up, Maeve, and stop asking questions." He leans down; my hands unconsciously tighten around the gutting knife. "Unless you want in there with him."

"No, sir," I say quickly, ducking my head.

I can almost feel his glare against my skin, but I won't look up. Finally, he stomps back to Uncle Lorcan, and they leave the shack. And I feel like I can breathe again. I peer behind me at the creature—at Silas. His appearance has loosened my lips. This is the first time I've ever dared to speak up against Dad. I'd questioned him, and his decisions. I'd almost done it twice, my lips poised to ask when we got into the business of capturing people, before I'd been cowed back into submission.

But it's always been that way. My cage may not have iron bars, but it's just as confining as our captive's.

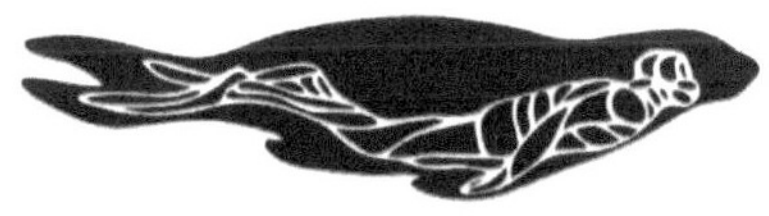

Sitting outside on a rickety wooden stool, I'm surrounded by a tangled web of netting that sprawls across my lap like seaweed. Dad and Uncle Lorcan are gone for the day, and I chance working outside the cottage today. The weather was fine, after all. It had nothing to do with Silas.

The rough fibers of the net scrape against my calloused hands as I mend the holes that were created by age and Uncle Lorcan's temper. There is a rhythm to it—pull, knot, tighten—but it's a dance of captivity, one I now share with the creature before me.

When he arrived two days ago, his skin glistened like scales, but now it appears duller and more human-like. The paleness lends to him being a vampire, I'd imagine, though I've never seen one of those either, only read of them. He keeps claiming he's a selkie, and I don't know if the scales are evidence in favor or against. Finfolk need to blend in. Staying shiny for days wouldn't help. But selkies are, essentially, seal people. They wear their seal pelt and shapeshift into a seal. Without it, they're human—and stuck. But I've never read about selkies having scales in their human form.

His eyes though, they stayed a swirling shifting gray, like liquid silver. Mine do the same sometimes, but in gold. You have to stare long enough to catch the movement, when my irises swirl. It usually happens when I'm overcome with emotion. It's a legacy I have left from Mama. But her eyes were like Silas', the golden color always moving.

"Is it gold, then?" Silas' voice breaks the lull of my thoughts.

My fingers twist in the nets and I look down at the weaving. "Is what gold?" Not *my* eyes, or Mama's. If they were, Dad or Uncle Lorcan would have figured out how to extract it.

"That which I could tempt you with," he explains.

I let out a breath, realizing he wasn't calling out my oddness, but returning to his desperate game from the first night, where he'd attempted to offer me anything in return for me releasing him.

"Perhaps you desire riches beyond measure?" he continues, those stormy eyes wide.

I can't help the laugh that escapes me. He's better off offering that to Dad than me. "What would I do with gold here?"

"Land? A title? Surely there must be something," he continues, his tone threaded with a thin layer of urgency.

"Land and title won't mend these nets," I remind him. They would only line Dad's pockets.

"Power, then. Power to change your fate," he says, his voice dropping to a hushed tone, as if the very words were sacred. It's nearly right, but not quite the key to the lock.

"Power is fleeting," I counter, my fingers never ceasing their dance among the ropes.

"Then what, Maeve? What is it you truly seek?" Silas leans forward in his cage, his expression earnest, eyes searching mine for an answer he could grasp. Those sharp features are pinched, worried. I can see him struggling to come up with another offer that might sway me.

For a moment, I consider sharing my story with him—the years of mistreatment at the hands of the only family I had left, the nights spent looking out at the unforgiving sea, wondering if Mama ever looked at the same sky from wherever she was. Wondering if her capture was still a better life than we had here. But I hold back, letting the thoughts churn inside me like a stormy tide.

"Absolutely nothing," I declare with finality, frowning at his persistence. "There is nothing that can be given to me while I'm here." Anything he can offer me is worthless compared to what I truly long for: a life outside my own invisible bars, one with support and love. But if I left, I would be alone, afraid. I don't belong here, but where else could I go?

"You are that dull, that predictable, that you'll live and die without considering there could be more out there for you," Silas spits at me, venom lacing each word.

"Apparently so," I say, even though I grit my teeth as I confirm it.

He stares at me, long enough that I can feel it like a physical touch. My focus flicks back to him and he's still staring. But not as though he's looking *for* something but looking *at* something.

I avert my gaze, his changed demeanor making me uncomfortable. That's likely what he wants. "What?" I finally demand.

"I've figured it out," he says softly, almost to himself, his voice tinged with quiet understanding that makes me pause.

"What have you figured out then?" I ask sharply, returning my focus to the task at hand.

"You desire the return of your mother."

I freeze, my hands still entwined in the nets as I meet Silas' intense gaze. I thought he'd *actually* figured it out. That he knew what was deep within the recesses of my heart, what I'd just let myself discover. My ache for freedom. Freedom he couldn't offer me, because if I left here, I'd have nothing and no one.

But Mama... he shouldn't even know of her.

"Explain yourself," I demand, my eyes narrowing in suspicion.

He shifts uncomfortably at my scowl, though that could be because he's in a cage. "I've heard them speak, your Uncle Lorcan and your father... their talk of her absence. Of the finborn." He huffs and drags a dirty finger over the bars, making them twang softly. "I may be trapped in this form, but I am not blind to the world around me."

I exhale slowly, releasing the tension that had coiled in my muscles as I resume my task of mending the nets. "Yes, well. That's not an option."

"So, I've discovered it, then?" he asks quietly. "This is what I can give you?"

"Your guess is irrelevant," I say, keeping my voice steady. "Even if you *were* right, how could you 'give' her to me?"

"Release me, Maeve," Silas says, his voice low. "Together, we can journey to Unseen Lake."

"Unseen Lake?" The words sound foreign on my tongue.

"I must find my pelt before the hunter's moon, or the cost will be... dire," he reminds me, a fervent glow igniting in his eyes. His hand stretches out, fingers grazing the air between us, beseeching. "I lost it in a scuffle with the finfolk, and it fell to depths of the Unseen Lake near their domain. But perhaps there, we may uncover traces of your mother."

My mind races with thoughts.

Could I really find her? After all these years, would my mother recognize the girl left behind, now a woman grown and clad in the armor of desperation?

If I found her, I wouldn't be alone. I'd have some support, some family, a *loving* family, again. I could start over with her by my side, *live* with her by my side. We could both start over. But... "What about the finfolk?"

He starts at that, his long fingers tightening around the bars. "What of them?" He frowns deeply, lines creasing and making his cheekbones look even sharper.

"They took her."

His quicksilver gaze focuses back on me, dragging over my face. "So, she'd be found *there* in the Unseen Lake, near my pelt. Then... you go there and find her. "

A spark of longing ignites within me, a desire for adventure and escape from my stifling life. It would be the freedom I longed for, what I read about in each water-stained book in the library, just in a different form.

But the idea is impossible.

"Words," I murmur dismissively, though my heart aches with the possibility. "Meaningless words, Silas. You'll get to the Lake and find your pelt and leave me alone with the finfolk. That isn't giving her to me but giving me another problem."

"Words," he agrees, nodding solemnly. "But also promises, if you dare to believe them. You come with me to the Unseen Lake, and we *will* find the finfolk before the full moon. And if your mother is there, we'll take her back. Before any trip to the selkies."

"You'll take me there? And not leave me to become a prisoner like my mother."

His nod is solemn, weighted. "You will not become like your mother."

Before I can respond, the door from the cottage bangs open with such violence that it seems the very hinges might surrender. Dad storms outside, his shadow overtaking me like an approaching storm cloud.

"Maeve!" he bellows, his face red as if the sea itself had slapped him.

"D-dad," I stammer, standing quickly and shuffling as far from Silas' cage as I can. He was meant to still be fishing, on the boat I still spy ahead of us in the water. He wasn't supposed to return for hours. "Did something happen to the boat?"

"No, fool girl," he snarls. "The sheep have broken through the fence again!"

"Dad, I—" My protest dies in my throat, knowing well the futility of explaining that I've been mending nets since dawn, that the sheep are not mine to tend.

"Just fix it before they destroy the turnip patch!" With a last glare that promises retribution, he retreats into the house, slamming the door behind him, leaving tremors in his wake.

I suppose it's only luck that he didn't notice my proximity to Silas, or the intensity in our conversation just before his arrival.

I turn back to Silas, the remnants of my father's anger dissipating like morning mist upon my resolve. My decision solidifies, fragile but resolute.

"Deal," I whisper, the word tasting of brine and possibilities. "We'll seek your pelt... and my mother at the Unseen Lake."

Triumph enters Silas' eyes, replacing the desperation that had been there before. In that moment, bound by promises as delicate as seafoam, we become allies.

Chapter 3

In their human guise, finfolk are said to be charming and persuasive, using their charisma to manipulate and deceive. The aquatic spouses, or 'mates,' of this species—merpeople who were bewitched or manipulated and transformed over time—typically remain hidden in the finfolk's underwater realm, often depicted as a shadowy and magical kingdom beneath the sea. Meanwhile,

> *the finborn—those born a fin-*
> *folk—roam the Aboveground*
> *in search of humans. Why hu-*
> *mans are their chosen prey re-*
> *mains unknown.*

-Excerpt from Beneath the Surface: Unveiling the Mysteries of Selkies and Finfolk.

Dad straightens his collar, adjusting it carefully in the hazy reflection of the front window. His gaze slides to the side, where I'm standing behind him, trying to look weak and frail.

"Gladys will be by to see you're up and about," he rumbles. "No daughter of mine will lie idle, sick or not. You best be mending those pants when she arrives."

My heart pounds against my ribs, fueled by equal parts dread and determination. Beads of sweat form on my forehead, a physical manifestation of my nervousness that I hope will add some validity to my lie. I consider coughing insincerely to add to the illusion of illness, but don't want to push my luck. That he's letting me stay home from church by myself is already a victory. Usually, he and Uncle Lorcan take turns accompanying me on Sundays. But with Lorcan away at sea, it's Dad's turn to sit in the pews and put on a show of being a respectable man. Normally, I sit stiffly between them, trying not to "embarrass" them by my mere existence. But when I'm sick, I'm banished to the back of the church with Gladys, the children's bible teacher. And now, with a fever spreading through the village after the recent storm, even Gladys will soon be absent as she cares for the quarantined children.

The deep chime of the bell echoes through the morning mist from somewhere down the lane. Dad sets off towards the church, closing the door with a thud behind him, sealing my fate with it. I hold my breath, waiting until his figure is swallowed by the foggy embrace of the cobblestone path leading to the town's edge. As soon as he disappears into the mist, I spring into action. There's no time for hesitation.

I tear through the cottage, our one-room shack, hands trembling as I gather essentials and throw them into a worn satchel: clothes for me, hastily grabbed garments for Silas, whose skin has been exposed to nothing but rough, threadbare fabric for too long. He won't last long in the woods like that. The air thickens with dust and the musty scent of old wood as I rummage through drawers and cupboards, their contents spilling onto the floor like cascading waterfalls of my meager life.

And then there's the trunk. Dad's prized possession. Uncle Lorcan's handiwork is still visible, jagged nails hammered into the splintered oak to 'restore' it after Mama was stolen. It used to be locked when I was a child, but the finborn had pried it open during their raid and taken Mama and everything else Dad valued within. Once Uncle Lorcan fixed it, Dad stopped locking it, as though he had nothing else of value to protect. Even so, I was never allowed to see what was inside. A shiver runs through my body, not out of fear, but the thrill of rebellion. I hesitate only for a heartbeat before flipping the heavy lid.

But instead of revealing the treasures or secrets I'd imagined, there's nothing particularly noteworthy inside. A few trinkets, a faded ribbon, some documents. I reach into the trunk and feel around its rough edges, hoping to find *something* of use buried beneath the layers of dust and neglect. My fingers brush against a pouch that jingles with the promise of freedom.

Yet I frown; I'd been doing the books since I was old enough to multiply sums and we were always scrimping. A hundred or more coins slip through my fingers, enough to have given me new clothes when I'd outgrown what was left of Mama's or repaired the hole in the fence with new wood instead of me needing to ransack the alleys for abandoned pieces that gave me splinters. With renewed irritation, I slip a few coins into my pocket. Quickly closing up the trunk, I shove it back into place.

The knapsack hangs across my shoulder as I survey the key to the cage that hangs openly against the scratched wall by Dad's bed. A symbol of control, so brazen in its placement, for who would dare defy him?

I grab it and head to the door. With the key secured, I steal one last glance at the empty hearth and my flat pallet beside it, the solitary chair, the piles of mending I had yet to finish. The mess I've made reminds me of when Mama was taken, but this time it is not a finborn coming to steal her away. It is me taking the selkie.

I sprint outside toward Silas' cage, my steps light. This is it, my first genuine act of rebellion. For Mother. For myself.

The key slides smoothly into the lock with a satisfying click and the door swings open. Silas emerges cautiously, like a pale and sinuous octopus stretching its limbs until he can stand tall. He blinks in confusion at his sudden freedom, his muscles tensing beneath his skin.

"Hurry," I urge, thrusting a bundle of clothes into his arms. Gladys will be here soon, gossiping her way through the village until she reaches our cottage.

He sneers down at the clothes in distaste. "This is stolen?" he questions with a disapproving scowl.

"Yes, and? Get dressed," I reply, trying to keep my voice low.

"This is... distasteful," he grumbles, his scowl deepening. "And illegal."

"So is kidnapping," I retort, glancing over my shoulder to make sure Gladys isn't approaching yet. "Are you honestly going to refuse them because they're stolen?"

"I am not one to shy away from the benefits." He sniffs dismissively, quickly slipping into the ill-fitting garments. "But I want it noted that I object to this method."

I roll my eyes, exasperated. I won't be telling him about the few coins at the bottom of my bag. "Just get dressed!"

Silas complies, the clothes hanging loosely on his lean frame but still a vast improvement from the tattered loincloth he had been wearing.

"Now, which way?" he asks when his skin is finally covered.

"Prism Lake lies south. That direction," I point towards the road leading away from the shore behind us, shouldering my makeshift pack filled with provisions. "But I'm not familiar with the path."

"Neither am I," Silas admits, furrowing his brow in thought. "The last thing I remember is being swallowed by darkness and waking up on the icy waters of the Northern Ocean."

"We need to be cautious," I warn, scanning our surroundings anxiously. "We don't want to attract any unwanted attention. No running into any-one."

"I am obviously a strong swimmer," he suggests. "We could travel by water."

"No!" I almost scream the word, and both of us dart our gazes around us to make sure no one heard. "No travel by water. Won't... won't that turn you shimmery again?"

Silas looks almost human now, except for his vampire-pale skin and unusual eyes. My own eyes are no better, but at least we don't sparkle like fish scales. The story of two odd-eyed travelers might be an interesting enough detail for the traders to spread during their routes; adding in evidence of a shapeshifter will just put him—or us—into an-other cage.

He raises an eyebrow, his silvery eyes skeptical. "Yes, if this human skin gets wet."

"Exactly. Which won't let you blend in." I nod, thinking quickly. "We need to stop by the village library first." It's absurd to even call it that, a room housing such a small collection of books that it hardly deserves the name. But it *does* have maps.

Silas offers no argument; he simply follows my lead as we slip into the shadowed alleys of our village.

"Will your family follow?" Silas asks, his voice barely above a whisper, as if even the slightest sound might reveal our location.

"They never came after Mama when she was taken," I murmur back, clinging to that slim thread of logic. "Maybe we'll be granted the same indifference."

"Perhaps," he says, though the skepticism lacing his tone suggests he finds little comfort in my words.

We glide like a sailboat in calm seas, smoothly skimming from building to building, always on the lookout for any signs of danger. "Stay alert," I remind Silas in a hushed voice, feeling the weight of my own words. This is more than just a desperate escape; it was the first genuine act of defiance I had ever dared to commit.

He nods subtly, his gray eyes sharp and vigilant, scanning every corner and alleyway where danger could hide. He moves with the grace and strength of a predator, every inch of him honed for survival.

In contrast, I'm nearly lumbering beside him, an oaf who can't tell up from down.

Finally, we reach the village library. The door groans on its hinges, a traitorous sound that seems far too loud in the hush of church hour. This room had been a secret escape in the rare moments I could slip my father's watchful eye. My fingers brush against the splintered wood, tracing the scars left by time and neglect. The air is thick with the musty odor of old paper and decaying wood, one that brings memories of reading about the other creatures in the world, not just the finfolk but the fae and sirens and dragons and mages, any creature I could find, so I wouldn't be caught unaware should a creature come to steal me away.

Now, I huff at the irony.

"Don't worry, we're not breaking in," I whisper to Silas, my voice a whisper as we slip inside. I ignore his growled complaint behind me.

The room is small, with barely enough space for two people to move around comfortably. I could spread my arms wide and reach both walls with ease. But despite its size, this is the largest collection of books in our village, the shelves packed tightly with volumes and stacks balanced precariously on top. They lean like the old men who never venture inside.

As we step carefully across the creaky floor-boards, I lead us along a familiar path to avoid any loose nails towards the back room. The air smells musty and old, a mixture of paper and dust that lingers on my skin. Bridgit, the volunteer librarian, has diligently kept track of the maps that are brought in by passing ships, hiding them away amongst the other books.

"Are all human books this decrepit?" Silas asks as he follows behind me.

I pause in my search, taking in the cluttered room around us, the walls lined with hundreds of well-loved stories. "Only the good ones," I reply. "It's a sign that they've been cherished."

"Or neglected," Silas says with a sniff.

"That too," I agree. "Here." I find what we need: a collection of maps, their edges frayed but still legible enough to guide us on our journey. We lay them out across the faded wallpaper, as there is no space for a table in this cramped room. Silas holds the corners while I trace my fingers over the lines and contours, searching for the safest route for our escape.

"We'll follow this stream," I murmur, pointing to the thin blue line that snakes away from the village, a delicate vein on the parchment. "It will keep us hidden... keep you safe from prying eyes. Just don't jump in."

Silas nods, committing the path to memory. "I'll blend in. Whatever it takes to reach the finfolk." He slides his quicksilver gaze to me and appears to be weighing whether to speak. "You know you will likely never return, spending the rest of your life without these humans by your side, in a place you've never seen and may never leave."

"I know," I answer softly. Leaving means severing ties with everything I've ever known, with the people who have raised me and the life that has been etched into every fiber of my being. It means stepping into the unknown. Finding something beyond the confined walls of this village, beyond the suffocating expectations that had bound me for so long. Finding my mother.

"There's nothing left for me here," I continue. "But if I find Mama? That's a new beginning."

And I won't be alone in this new world, I'll have Mama.

"And if it doesn't work out that way?" he asks quietly.

"Then at least I tried."

Silas nods, his expression unreadable as he absorbs my words. "Very well. Then let's not waste any more time here," he says, folding up the maps with precision. "We'll follow the stream, stay hidden and get you to the finfolk."

Carefully, we return each map to its place on the shelves, leaving no trace of our desperate search behind. As silently as we entered, we slip back into daylight, accompanied by distant hymns as we make our escape.

Chapter 4

Once a human is captured by a finborn, they are taken to the underwater domain where their fate is determined by those who captured them. In many cases, they become a finborn's spouse, regardless of their gender. Like the aquatic spouses, they are expected to be subservient and join the finborn's harem. Alternatively, if not chosen for marriage, the human may become a servant or

> *'Bonded' individual, fulfilling various roles within the fin-folk community. This status, while less prestigious, still involves a permanent place within the finfolk's hierarchy.*
>
> -Excerpt from Beneath the Surface: Unveiling the Mysteries of Selkies and Finfolk.

"What else do you remember?"

We've been traveling for hours, the village now a mere speck in the distance behind us. We found the stream only recently, and water rushes over smooth rocks, drowning out all other sounds. Silas has been staring into the water silently since we found it, gazing at it with a longing that feels almost uncomfortable to watch.

He drags his attention from the stream to me. "Beg pardon?" he asks gruffly. The wind tugs at his white hair, sending strands dancing around his face.

The bright whiteness catches the fading light, and for an odd moment, I wonder what it would be like to run my fingers through it—if it would feel like the seaweed Mama used to find on the shore or like the tangled nets I repair every day. I shake the thought away.

"You said the last thing you remembered was waking up in the ocean," I explain. "So... what else do you remember?"

His eyes dart back to the small stream, and he looks to be deciding whether to answer me. "Does it matter?"

"Probably not," I admit. "But we've got another day and a half's walk. Given how chatty you were in the cage, I assumed we'd talk a little."

"I was trying to convince you to release me. I would have said anything, spoken until my voice was hoarse if needed." Silas glances up, his expression unchanged. "We need to stay focused, Maeve. We've both agreed to this trip and the full moon is five nights away. *Chatting* is a luxury we can't afford."

"It will make it go faster," I tell him, almost wheedling. He remains silent as I consider how to convince him to talk to me. I spent years talking to myself or getting yelled at by Dad and Uncle Lorcan. I wasn't game to continue the tradition.

"Consider it a… *societal* rule. Making conversation, being polite."

"A societal rule?" he asks, his thin brows raising.

"Yes, you like rules, right? Making conversation on a journey is practically a law."

He frowns, considering it. "Very well. You asked what I remembered before ending up in your father's net. I remember being home. Being… worried. I remember thinking there would be consequences." He pauses, his jaw clenching. "And then cold, the icy grip of water not my home."

"Consequences of what?" I ask softly, watching his silver eyes shift and swirl with something dark.

He lets out a sigh as heavy as the ocean. "We come of age when we're twenty-five and must complete a task. I didn't do it, so…"

"So… they knocked you unconscious and tossed you into the sea," I finish, my brow furrowing in confusion.

"It was more like a prank," he says with a shrug, but there was a hint of bitterness in his voice.

"Right," I say skeptically. I may not have much experience with people but even I know what's a good natured joke and what is attempted murder. "What was the task?"

"A, ah, a kind of ritual," he says, stuttering slightly. "How you choose to complete the ritual decides your fate in the clan, whether you're to be given respect."

None of the books I've read ever talked about the specifics of creature societies. *Beneath the Surface* might have, but any mention would have been the parts of the book Dad took from me. Silas' caginess makes me not want to pry further and cause tension with the creature I'm relying on to help save my mother. Still, I can't help but ask, "Why didn't you do it? The ritual."

Silas waves his hand dismissively, clearly trying to downplay his failure. "I just wasn't interested in it, not a moral issue, really," he begins, his voice tinged with a hint of defiance. I can see the shadows of doubt flickering in his eyes, as if he's trying to convince not only me but himself as well.

I raise an eyebrow. "Not interested in a coming-of-age tradition that could determine your place in society?"

He shrugs nonchalantly. But before he can continue, a loose rock under his foot, combined with Dad's ill-fitting shoes, sends him stumbling forward. With a startled cry, he falls to the ground, clutching his leg where a deep gash has formed from the fall.

I rush to his side, helping ease him to a moss-covered stone beside the water while he releases a stream of curses more colorful than Uncle Lorcan on his worst night. Blocking out the sound, I rummage through my small knapsack, retrieving a thin roll of bandages and a vial of soothing salve. Silas winces as I begin to clean the wound, his jaw clenching against the sting, but at least he's not screeching anymore.

"You were saying about the tradition," I prompt gently, trying to distract him from the discomfort.

Silas' gaze fixes on the bubbling stream in front of us. "It's not that I wasn't interested in tradition per se," he begins, his voice softer now. "It's just... It felt like a cage. A way to box us into predetermined roles."

"And instead you ended up in a literal cage," I reply dryly.

Silas lets out a low chuckle, the sound carrying a hint of bitterness as he meets my eyes. "Indeed," he concedes. "I didn't like the roles. But I've rethought things. The abduction cleared my mind a bit. I'm not... not giving up just yet."

I continue to tend to his wound, applying the salve. The earthy scent of the forest mixes with the herbal fragrance of the salve. It's... calming. Silas watches me work in silence.

"We bleed the same," I say idly as I wipe my hands free of his iron-rich blood.

"Did you think we wouldn't?" he asks, resting his palms against the rock and leaning back to stare down at me.

I wrap the bandage around his leg. "You're a sea creature," I explain. "The books back home talk about how different creatures are from humans, but they're not specific. I thought, perhaps, we had different blood, is all."

"You think I'd bleed blue like the water then?" he asks, shifting slightly, the corners of his eyes crinkling with amusement. "Then vampires must bleed black—"

"Because of the death," I continue. "Sure. And werewolves—"

"Yellow," he finishes.

My hands pause on his leg, and I cock my neck up towards him. "Why yellow instead of silver?"

"The warmth of the moonlight, something to be loved rather than feared," he says with a smile.

I laugh. "That sounds poetic. Better than what the books said. All about savagery and weakness for silver."

"What did they say about water creatures?"

"Not much," I admit, returning my attention to his leg. "The one book still left in the library says finfolk are vicious and mean shapeshifters who steal human spouses and kill mermaids." I offer him a strained, apologetic smile. "Selkies are barely more than prey, easily duped and manipulated by humans."

He smirks back at me, an expression looking just as strained. "You manipulated me right out of my cage."

"Which is why," I continue, trying to avoid repeating the even more unflattering things the books said about selkies, "I like the poetry of your idea rather than the folklore from the books."

"Folklore results from stories, not truths," he muses, his eyes scanning the surrounding forest. "But the stories we tell do shape our world in their own way."

I nod, finishing up the bandaging and returning to our conversation before his tumble. "And you didn't want to be shaped by that tradition."

He meets my gaze, his eyes intense yet vulnerable. "I wanted to shape my path. But now here I am, on a path I didn't expect. Things have a way of working out."

Silence settles between us like a thick fog. His silver eyes continue shifting and I wonder if the gold in mine is doing the same. After a minute, I clear my throat.

"What color do you think dragons bleed?" I ask.

Silas leans back again, his gaze drifting up to the sky where soft light filters through the leafy canopy. It makes him look almost ethereal, like the magical creature he is.

"Gold," he muses after a moment, his eyes alight with imagination. "A molten river of liquid gold that flows from their wounds, casting a shimmering glow upon the earth."

"Gold it is then," I declare with a grin, securing the bandage in place before sitting back on my heels. "There. That should do for now."

Silas nods gratefully, his eyes lingering on mine for a moment longer than necessary. "Thank you."

"Of course," I say. "We're together in this."

The sun drops low in the sky, painting everything in a dusky orange glow. We settle beside the stream, finding a spot under the thick canopy of a tree.

I stretch out my legs and lean back against the tree trunk, breathing in the fresh, cool air. The entire day still feels like a dream; that I broke Silas out, that I'd run away from home.

I've also been walking more than I ever had. My household chores didn't prepare me for this. Earlier, there'd been a fork in the path, one that claimed to be a more direct route to Prism Lake, and I'd all but begged to take it, fearing for my feet. But the sign said it was off limits except to carriages and motor coaches. Silas refused to take the shortcut, insisting that the rules must be followed.

Half-heartedly, I scowl over at him. He appears fine from the day's walk, not even winded.

"Do we have provisions?" he asks, digging through my hastily packed bag. His white hair falls messily over his forehead, and he shakes it back, revealing those sharp cheekbones and strong jawline. He withdraws a cloth covered pack of jerky and wrinkles his nose. "Never mind, I'll find a fish." And he stands and stalks towards the stream before I have a chance to answer.

I watch the long line of his back bent over the dark water and restrain a shiver. At the water, not him, of course. I quickly distract myself gathering dry leaves to build a fire for the fish. My fingers fumble with the flint and firestriker, the small metal tool shaped like a thick fishhook, sparks flicking until they finally catch on the tinder. Flames lick hungrily at the wood and the small alcove brightens.

"Here's dinner, he says, brandishing a fish. But when he sees the fire, the fish falls to the ground with a thud. He recoils, his eyes wide with terror.

"Fire!" His voice cracks, raw with fear. He stumbles back, tripping over the protruding roots of our alcove, his gaze locking on the blaze as if it were a predator come to life.

"Please," he gasps, his breaths short and panicked. "Make it stop."

"Okay, okay," I soothe, dropping to my knees to smother the flames with the dirt. The fire dies under my hands and the glow that brought warmth to my cheeks now recedes into a harmless wisp of smoke. "It's going out. See? You're safe."

His eyes flicker nervously towards the smoke as if it was a sentient being poised to attack. "Thank you," he whispers.

"It's okay," I tell him, standing to reach out a hand to touch his arm. "What happened?"

He shakes off my touch, lowering himself to the ground, his muscles coiled with tension, his eyes distant as if lost in haunting memories.

I sit beside him. "I'm sorry," I whisper, unsure of how to comfort him in the face of such a primal terror. "You don't have to talk about it if you don't want to."

Silas shakes his head, his jaw clenched in determination. "All my kind... we fear fire. It consumes us in ways you cannot understand," he confesses, his voice a thread, fraying and thin. "Our essence is bound to the water; fire sears our souls, strips us of our freedom."

His pale cheeks flush with pink and he avoids eye contact, reaching back for the fish and dusting off the dirt.

Selkies, the shapeshifters of the ocean, caught between land and tide, forever yearning for the call of the waves. How cruel that the flicker of a simple flame could instill such dread in a creature.

"I'm afraid of water," I say, wanting to offer something of myself in return.

He looks up at me, his brow furrowing, confusion mingling with curiosity. "Water?" he echoes. "You?"

I nod, a faint smile blooming. It is funny, the fisher's daughter who won't dip a toe in the surf. "Yes, water. I was never allowed in it as a child. Mama refused," I explain. "I never learned to swim. And so it... terrifies *me* in a way I can't explain. The vastness of it, the unknown depths and relentless power... it's suffocating."

"What irony that you're afraid of water," he murmurs, more to himself than to me.

I shrug. I'd already thought the same, this silly fisher's daughter.

I reach out tentatively, my hand finding his where it rests on the grass. His skin is cool to the touch, a reminder of his ties to the sea. He doesn't pull away this time, his eyes meeting mine with a vulnerability that takes my breath away.

"I'm sorry for scaring you," I tell him, squeezing his hand.

"I'm sorry for screaming," he responds quietly. "Thank you for putting it out so quickly."

As the last rays of sunlight filter through the leaves, casting a golden glow over our sanctuary by the stream, I find myself wanting to share more of my story with Silas. To peel back the layers of my past and reveal the scars that have shaped me into the person sitting beside him now. To offer more of myself, like he's offered himself today.

I'm about to tell him of my dreams of the water, the indefinable pull towards the horizon when he looks down at our joined hands. A flicker of something unnameable passes through his eyes before he gently extricates his hand from mine. His gaze shifts back to the fish in his lap.

"We should eat," he suggests, avoiding my eyes. "The moon will soon rise, and we have a long journey ahead."

"Of course," I say, wiping my hand on my skirt to remove the sensation of his skin lingering on it. And then I understand what he just said, and my lips curl up in disgust. "Selkies eat fish raw?"

And he laughs.

Chapter 5

In contrast to the finfolk, selkies are known as more genial shapeshifters. By shedding their seal skin, they can assume a human form, allowing them to walk on land, interact with humans, and experience life outside the sea. Conversely, donning their seal skins allows them to return to their aquatic world where they are skilled swimmers and have an innate connection to the ocean's depths.

> -Excerpt from Beneath the Surface: Unveiling the Mysteries of Selkies and Finfolk.

The next day drags on as we push our way through the thick underbrush of the woods. The branches reach out to snag at our clothing, and we have to carefully maneuver around them, making slow progress through the dense forest. If we're lucky, we might just reach Prism Lake by tomorrow midday, even if that means another night spent sleeping under the stars. After decades of sleep curled by the ashes, I wouldn't mind it much.

As the light fades once again, I break the silence that settled between us since our last meal, another dinner of raw fish caught from the stream and my jerky.

"Have you ever seen the Nightshimmer butterflies during a full moon?" I ask.

It's not much in the way of conversation—not that I've had much opportunity for practice—but it's better than nothing.

"They say their wings glow with the light of a thousand captured stars," I add.

Silas responds in his deep rumbling voice. "Never heard of them."

"Not at all? Or just during the full moon?" I press. His shrug is enough of an answer and I frown. "According to the books, they should be all over Prism Lake, pollinating the hydroponic flowers. Right beside the main selkie settlement."

"I spend little time above the surface," he mutters. "And you can't always trust what you read in books. Tales have a way of getting twisted over time."

My lips purse in disappointment. I suppose it shouldn't surprise me that the scant books from our tiny village library might not hold the whole truth. There's so much of the world I've never seen, and Silas' offhanded dismissal only sharpens that realization. I glance down at the stream, the silver sheen of the water reflecting the twilight sky, and try to shake the inadequacy creeping over me.

Still, I refuse to let the silence stretch too long. It feels like something opened up between us yesterday, and I want to tease at that new connection. My first one, save what I barely had with Dad and Uncle Lorcan. "You know, I've never been this far from home before," I say, stepping carefully over a cluster of roots.

Silas doesn't look up, but his brow furrows slightly. "I guessed that," he replies, his voice soft against the gurgle of the water.

The bluntness of his response makes me smile faintly. "Is this the farthest you've been from your home too?"

His swirling eyes slide over to me, unreadable as ever. "I didn't choose this trip, you'll recall."

"I know. It was just a question." I pause, adjusting the strap of my pack. "What's it like?" I ask, trying to keep the curiosity in my voice light. "Your home, I mean."

He hesitates, his gaze flicking back to the water as if searching for the right answer among the ripples. "It's... vast," he begins, his tone thoughtful. "Dark, yet alive with light. The currents move like veins, carrying life to every corner. There's beauty in it, but also danger. You learn to read the tides, to understand the balance."

I blink, trying to picture it—a world so different from my own. "It sounds beautiful."

"It can be."

"And the finfolk domain?" I ask, almost hesitantly, not sure I'm ready for the answer.

He pauses, his steps slowing as his gaze drifts toward the horizon, though the dense forest obscures it. His voice, when he speaks, is quieter, almost guarded. "The finfolk domain... suffice it to say, you will have a difficult time."

"Oh?"

He chuckles, the sound surprisingly warm, though it carries a sharp edge. "Your fear of water will be the troublesome part there. You realize they live fully underwater?"

I blanch, the weight of his words hitting me like an icy wave. I didn't remember that detail from my clandestine readings. "It will be fine. We'll just... blend in. Underwater." I say, huffing a laugh. "Two finborn, one with scales and strange eyes, and the other... also with strange eyes and a fear of water."

"You... don't need to accompany me," he says quietly, his tone softer than I expect.

"I do," I reply, searching for that same confidence that somehow pushed me to release him from his cage and leave my home. "We're in this now. The shapeshifter without his pelt and the fisher's daughter, planning to infiltrate a den of monsters."

He hums thoughtfully and returns his attention to the stream. "They're not all monsters, you know," he says, more to the water than to me.

"Finfolk?"

"Yes. What did you say you read yesterday? That finfolk are all vicious killers," he says, slashing his arm across a whip-thin branch. I have to duck to avoid the boomerang back. "That's... not all of them."

I furrow my brow, trying to understand the sudden sharpness in his tone. "Sure, but their society is built on stealing humans," I say hesitantly. *Like my mother* remains unsaid. "Maybe it's not all... ritualized, but it's still awful."

"Humans steal selkies. They bind them to the land by taking their pelts and force them to bear half-human children. The selkies are then left with the impossible choice of staying with their child or seeking their pelt and freedom," Silas counters sharply. "That's 'awful.'"

"But just because there are some bad actors doesn't mean every human is guilty of capturing a selkie," I argue back. "The stories portray every finborn as a kidnapper. But like you said," I continue, trying to calm the conversation down, "maybe those stories aren't entirely accurate."

"Maybe," Silas murmurs, kicking a stone out of our path.

The tension between us lingers as we continue walking, but I catch a flicker of something softer in his expression before he looks away. I glance at the stream again, the faint sound of its flow masking my unsteady breathing. For now, the conversation settles, though the questions it raises churn like the water, refusing to still.

Just as I begin to relax, a faint sound catches my attention. I freeze, tilting my head to listen. Silas hears it too. He stops beside me, his swirling eyes narrowing as his body tenses. Without speaking, we exchange wary glances.

Pushing through thick undergrowth, we suddenly come upon a vibrant clearing where a colorful array of caravans, flags fluttering in the gentle breeze, and performers setting up tents in the fading light.

"A circus," I gasp, my eyes widening. I grip onto Silas' shirt sleeve and tug excitedly. "They came north once. I couldn't go but I saw the lights from our cottage. It sounded magical."

And it is. We watch in silence as acrobats practice their daring routines, clowns paint on bright smiles, and exotic animals yawn and stretch in their cages.

"What is *that*?" Silas asks.

I follow his gaze to the shiny metal automobile sitting just outside the circle of caravans. "Oh, I guess if you have spent little time with humans, you'd not have heard of them. No one in our village could afford one yet, but they're carriages powered by this kind of combustion. You can go miles and miles in only minutes."

"Humans are an odd bunch," Silas says under his breath.

"Unless we're trained as mages, we don't have magic or anything like you do," I tell him, feeling oddly protective of my species. "We've got to compete somehow." He's lucky I don't tell him the combustion is just controlled fire, at least according to the book I read.

Silas pulls his arm out of my grasp, his expression serious. "We'll go around," he declares.

We cautiously backtrack and circle around the clearing. However, just as we are about to make our way back to our original path, a low rumble of thunder echoes overhead and dark clouds quickly gather, blocking out the setting sun.

Quickening our pace, we try to outrun the storm but within seconds, the sky opens up and unleashes a heavy downpour upon us. My cloak quickly becomes weighed down with water, clinging to me like a suffocating second skin.

"Curse it!" Silas spits out, his voice barely audible above the roar of the rain. "We should have taken the stream—we would have been at the Lake by now."

I shake my head, the cold droplets snaking their way down my neck. "The water," I remind him, and he nods gravely. We both know that swimming through the stream is not an option for me.

"We need to find shelter," I shout through the haze of raindrops pelting down on us. Silas frowns then shrugs, or something close to it. It's difficult to see through the onslaught of water trying to drown us both. If we don't get him out of the rain soon, all my efforts in keeping his selkie scales concealed will be for naught.

"There are no settlements for miles," Silas says. He's right; the lack of villages and people along this branch of the stream was why we'd chosen it, after all.

Just as we're about to turn back and search for an alternative route, a voice calls out from behind us. Surprised, we turn to see a hazy blond man standing there, smiling with brilliantly white teeth against golden—now wet—skin.

"Excuse me," he begins politely. "But have you spotted a circus around here? I seem to have lost my way and can't find my encampment."

Silas looks ready to answer and send him away, but I grab hold of his arm, a plan forming in my mind. "We could stay in a caravan."

He frowns down at me. "Is that not breaking and entering?"

"No, Mr. Rulebook. We could offer to *trade* for shelter with him," I hiss, hoping my voice conveys more competence than I feel.

Silas drags his attention slowly across the man's appearance, taking in what I'd already seen, the worn and tattered clothes that haven't been properly mended. There is a hint of curiosity in the stranger's piercing blue eyes, matching the smirk on his lips.

"You can't trust everyone so blindly," he says. "Everyone has their own agenda, Maeve. And it may involve harming you."

"We're the ones with an agenda," I remind him. "A bed. *You* would certainly appreciate a warm bed after sleeping in a cage for so many days," I whisper, trying to entice Silas into agreeing.

His gaze flicks upwards towards the darkening sky. "We're running out of time."

"We have to stop, anyway." It's a testament to my exhaustion that I don't remind him of the shortcut we missed because of his rigidity towards rules, which would have probably already gotten us to Prism Lake without plunging into a stream.

Silas frowns and I wonder if he's thinking the same thing. Finally, when my skin is completely soaked through, he nods wearily, and I step forward.

"It's just back through those trees," I tell the man, pointing in the direction we came from. "But perhaps you'd be interested in a deal. We can offer our mending services in exchange for shelter from this rain for the night."

The man's grin widens, sparks of mischief lighting up his eyes. "Now that sounds like a fair trade indeed. Show me where the circus is, and I'll take you to a dry spot."

Together, we traipse through the pouring rain back to where we came from. The once lively clearing is now deserted, everyone seeking refuge from the downpour. From there, the man leads us through a maze of colorful caravans until we reach one that's double the length of my cottage, marked by a beautiful portrait of a blonde-haired green-eyed woman. The man gestures towards it and Silas and I both let out appreciative murmurs before he opens the door.

As we step inside, the caravan gently sways with the force of the rain against its roof. The interior is filled with warmth and comfort, thanks to thick rugs and tapestries woven with gleaming gold and silver threads. Soft pillows and cushions line the benches, inviting us to sink into their embrace.

However, as we settle in, I realize just how cramped the space is. It's more like an overcrowded storage room than a place for living creatures. Books, pillows, and statues are crammed into every available inch.

"I'll gather the mending supplies," the man says before disappearing into the back of the caravan, which is almost completely shrouded in darkness.

"Welcome, weary travelers," a voice greets us from within the dimness.

Silas and I exchange puzzled glances as we strain to make out anything in the sea of objects surrounding us. Finally, our eyes adjust to the low light, focusing on the source: a woman draped in flowing robes. It is the same woman depicted on the front of the caravan, but now she appears lifelike, except she's ageless. While the painted woman looked a few years older than me, this woman could be twenty or she could be seventy. She sits before a small table covered in an intricately embroidered cloth, candles flickering atop it. Piles of books and stacks of paper crowd her surroundings like loyal attendants.

"It seems you seek refuge from the storm," she speaks with a knowing smile, gesturing towards us with graceful pale fingers. Her face is serene, with soft lines etched around her eyes and mouth. "But you carry more than just damp clothes and tired hearts. Secrets cling to your skin like the chill of this night."

Silas eyes the woman with a hint of suspicion, while I try to mask my unease with a polite smile.

"Come, come," she says.

After exchanging hesitant glances, we maneuver our way through the cluttered objects to sit on a low bench beside her table. With her permission, we push aside tapestries, herb satchels, and—inexplicitly—a pie to make room.

The woman leans closer, her eyes shimmering in the candlelight. "Allow me to offer you a glimpse into your intertwined fates," she murmurs, her voice almost hypnotic. "Beware the shadows that dance on your path, for they may lead you astray. Trust not in what you see but in what lies beneath."

Her gaze moves to Silas, her emerald eyes seeming to bore into our very souls. "One of you seeks what is missing, while the other is blind to the truths that surround you," she continues, her voice a melodious echo in the close confines of the caravan.

Silas shifts uncomfortably beside me, his gaze flickering towards the door as if considering a quick escape.

"The past will resurface, revealing what was lost," the woman continues. "Betraying trust can lead to darkness where there was once light."

Silas clears his throat, a nervous tension radiating from him. "Thank you for your insight," he manages to say, his voice strained.

She turns her gaze to me. "You carry the weight of a thousand unspoken words." As she reaches out and takes my hand gently in hers, a warmth spreads through me in the dimly lit caravan. Her touch is almost comforting in this strange space, like finding something safe in an unknown world. "Remember," she whispers, her voice soft yet filled with a haunting power, "the ties that bind you are stronger than you realize."

Silas' jaw tightens and he shifts uneasily in his seat. "Thank you for the shelter, Miss—"

She raises a thin blonde brow and drops my hand. "Amara," she says simply.

He tips his head. "Miss Amara. But we're not interested in parlor tricks or cryptic fortunes," he says, his voice sharp with irritation. "We'll just wait out the rain and be on our way once it lets up."

Amara's smile doesn't waver. "As you wish," she says. "But remember this! In each other's reflection, you will find the—"

"Miss Amara," Silas says, trying to cut her off. The caravan lurches slightly as a gust of wind rattles against its wooden walls.

"No need to prevaricate dear boy," Amara says. "The threads of fate are delicate things, easily tangled and broken."

Silas' irritation is clear in his voice as he interrupts again. "Thank you," he says dryly. "But, please. We need no more—"

"But indeed," she says, snapping her fingers. "Listen well to the water, for they carry the truths you seek."

A vein appears in Silas' forehead, clenching in time with the relentless rain beating down on the caravan's roof. "Miss Amara, plea—"

She slams her hands on the table, causing me to jump in surprise. "The choices you make now will shape your destiny together or apart," she declares.

Silas turns to me, his eyes wide with confusion and concern. "What is happening?" he mutters under his breath. "Is there not some societal rule here to stop her from speaking?"

"The truths you seek may hide in plain sight," she adds undeterred, "waiting to be uncovered."

Before we can utter another word, the man reappears from the shadows, holding a pile of clothes and a sharp needle and thread. He passes them to me with a chuckle. "Stop teasing them,

Amara," he scolds before turning to us. "Don't mind her. Amara's the circus' fortune teller. She doesn't always turn it off."

As if a candle has been extinguished inside her, Amara drops the eerie tone in her voice and her face loses its intense expression. She chuckles softly, her voice now playful and mischievous. "Sorry, can't help myself sometimes. It's fun to get carried away."

Silas visibly relaxes at her explanation, likely thinking that Amara's words were likely just part of her act. I, however, can't shake the feeling that there was more to her cryptic advice than mere theatrics.

Amara gestures to the man. "In case he hasn't introduced himself, this is Kael, my assistant."

Kael claps Silas on the shoulder. "While your girl does the mending, check out my closet. I have a shirt that might fit better, if you'll come with me."

Silas nods without clarifying that I'm *not* his girl, and the two disappear into the shadows of the caravan. I wash away the prickle under my skin at the thought of such a connection with Silas and settle into my seat to work on my part of the bargain. But as I start to work on the mending, my mind keeps drifting back to Amara's overly dramatic fortunes. The needle is heavy in my hand, the thread twisting and turning like the tangled threads of fate she mentioned.

Amara watches me quietly for a moment before speaking up. "You have a gentle touch," she says, her voice light and free of any hidden meanings this time. "Few have the patience for such delicate work."

I glance up at her, taken aback by the sincerity in her words. A warmth spreads through me at her unexpected praise and I offer a small smile in response. "Thank you."

She returns it warmly, the corners of her eyes crinkling. "You and Silas make quite an interesting pair," she remarks, casting a fleeting glance towards where Silas and Kael had disappeared earlier.

A selkie and a human on a journey to the finfolk, it certainly is an unconventional duo.

"That we do," I say, the warmth of the caravan and Amara's less ominous presence making me more at ease.

"There is more to your journey than meets the eye," she says cryptically, her tone turning somber once again.

I pause in my mending. "What do you mean?"

She meets my gaze, her eyes searching mine. "You both carry burdens that are not your own," she explains, her words hanging heavy in the air between us. "Do remember what I said, dear."

I swallow hard as a prickle of unease crawls up my spine. "Was all that not just part of your performance."

Amara leans back in her chair, her robes rustling softly. "No, girl. I may not usually let my words bleed from me as though I've been wounded, but I *say nothing* that isn't true."

The sound of rain against the roof intensifies, drowning out any further conversation. Silas and Kael return from the shadows, Silas now wearing another shirt, worn but dry and not as ill-fitting as Dad's.

"I appreciate the shirt," he says curtly, avoiding looking at Amara.

She smiles knowingly. "It was my pleasure, dear boy."

Tension hangs thick in the air inside the caravan, mirroring the storm raging outside.

Finally, I clear my throat. "Thank you again for your hospitality," I say. Better to brush past the implications from everything she's said tonight. "We're grateful for your kindness in allowing us shelter from the storm."

Amara's eyes gleam with satisfaction. "And Kael and I will appreciate having no holes in my good robes."

After another hour of my mending and Silas stewing in silence, Amara and Kael lead us through the rest of the caravan, which is just as cluttered as the front.

"We only have the one spare bed," Amara explains, gesturing to a corner where a large cot is covered in plush pillows and warm blankets. With all the clutter, there isn't even enough space for one of us to lie on the floor. "But it is cozy," she adds as if that's a selling point. "And it will keep you dry and safe through the night."

Silas shoots me a quick glance before reluctantly making his way towards the cot. I follow, feeling a mix of apprehension and curiosity swirling inside me like a storm of emotions. As we settle down on the cot, our shoulders barely touching, I can sense Silas' discomfort.

For me, it's less discomfort and more... unease, but a good unease. Like how my stomach felt with Michael Earlander used to smile at me when we were teenagers nearly grown. And when Sam Chapman kissed me behind the church when I turned thirteen. Before Dad scared them both away.

"Still believe this is better than sleeping on the ground?" he asks dryly.

I shift to get a better view of Silas, letting the memories drown deep within. The faint light filtering through a crack in the curtains illuminates his profile. "If I have to choose between being soaked by rain while lying on muddy ground or sharing a cot with you, I'll choose the cot."

He lets out a soft huff, his breath tickling my face. "High praise."

I roll my eyes teasingly. "Don't let it get to your head. I'd share a cot with a basket of eels if it meant staying dry."

While possibly true, it's still a bit of a fish tale. My bed has always been empty, a small and cold pallet by the hearth. A basket of eels might have been nice, for the loneliness. But a basket of eels wouldn't feel as nice as Silas. If he turned slightly, the hard planes of his chest would be pressing against mine. I swallow the thought before it shows on my face.

Silas chuckles softly, the sound vibrating through the small space between us. "I'll try not to take it personally." After another beat, he adds, "I thought sharing a bed was frowned upon by humans."

My cheeks heat and I pray to the fae the dim light hides it. "When they're together, certainly. It's looked down upon by society if they aren't married. At least in my village. But it isn't a law, or even a rule." I start to ramble and desperately want to shut myself up. "You know, some villages don't even believe in marriage. And that's just for humans. The books say other creatures—"

A roar of thunder interrupts me and I take the hint, clearing my throat. "So, yes, frowned upon but not a rule."

"A malleable societal rule," Silas muses, as if he's turning the thought over in his head. "Like Miss Amara continuing to speak when asked *repeatedly* to refrain," he adds dryly.

We fall silent again, the only sound the drumming of rain against the roof. The gentle sway of the caravan creates a soothing rhythm that lulls my senses but the reminder of Amara's words roll through my mind. I steal another glance at Silas, wondering if he's pondering them too.

He fidgets beside me, his fingers tapping a restless beat on the edge of the cot. Without thinking, I reach out and place my hand on top of his, stilling his nervous movements. He looks at me, surprise flickering across his features before settling into a quiet calm. The storm outside rages on, but inside the caravan, a different kind of tension coils between us.

"Thinking about what she said?" I ask softly.

He hesitates for a minute, as if weighing his words carefully. "I don't like seers."

"Why not?"

"They always speak in riddles," Silas continues with a touch of bitterness. "Promising truths that are never straightforward. There are no rules for them to abide by, they can simply spew their words and we're left to deal with the aftermath."

I nod in understanding, my thumb rubbing small circles on the back of his hand. "Do you believe there's truth in what she said?"

Silas gazes at me, his expression unreadable. "What do you think she meant?" he asks, his tone softer now.

One of you seeks what is missing, while the other is blind to the truths that surround you, she said. I know what I'm missing: Mama. But what truth is he blind to? And how are our fates tangled? What ties bind us?

If I take her clues to heart, it tells me he needs to realize something and then... maybe... maybe our story will continue, together.

I clear my throat, imagining how our story could continue. "I'm not sure," I admit as the rain pounds against the roof of the caravan, my voice barely audible over its clamor. "But... maybe we should keep her words in mind. Just in case."

Silas' jaw tightens, a flicker of apprehension crossing his features. "Do you really believe there's more to it?"

A loud crack of thunder interrupts our conversation, followed by a blinding flash of lightning that illuminates our small space. I flinch at the sudden brightness. As the thunder rumbles in the distance, his arm wraps around my shoulders instinctively, pulling me closer to him. His heartbeat thuds against my ear, a steady rhythm that matches the drumming of rain on the caravan roof.

I turn my head slightly to look at him, our eyes meeting in the dim light. "We'll find out," I tell him, my breath mingling with his. "When we get to the finfolk and when we find your pelt."

His grip tightens around me, almost uncomfortably, before he releases. "Yes, we will." He shifts until we're lying side by side again. "But for now, let us rest."

And I close my eyes, listening to the soothing sound of his breathing blending with the rain.

Chapter 6

Unlike finfolk, who are born in their amphibious form, selkie children are born as humans, a milestone that signals their initial integration into the terrestrial world. In contrast to their fully aquatic counterparts, these young selkies lead human lives until they begin to engage with their aquatic environment. As they spend significant time submerged, their latent seal skin begins to emerge in a remark-

> *able metamorphosis. It is a process that marks their physical transition from human to selkie: a true embodiment of their dual nature as creatures of both land and sea.*
>
> -Excerpt from Beneath the Surface: Unveiling the Mysteries of Selkies and Finfolk.

The next morning, we wake to the rain finally gone. Our bodies strayed together during sleep, the cot's slight size making it inevitable. Silas wastes no time in getting up, nearly vaulting from the cot, his eyes fixed on the door.

"Thank you for your hospitality, Miss Amara, Kael," he says as he moves towards the exit. "We must go, Maeve," he adds, voice low but laced with an edge that doesn't invite argument.

As I rise and step out of the caravan after Silas, Amara calls out, "Remember, child, the truths you seek may be closer than you think."

I turn back to give her a polite smile and then chase after Silas as he treks through the caravans.

We pass by the various performers setting up for the day, weaving through the crowd, sidestepping a fire-eater practicing with unlit swords. This is a human circus, meaning it should all be smoke and mirrors, games of distraction—until my gaze snags on something real near the outskirts of the circus grounds.

In a cage off to the side is a wolf, its sleek black fur glistening in the morning sun. Its coat, a tapestry of darkness, bristles as it moves with a predator's grace, yet there was no mistaking the weariness in its slumped shoulders. Its eyes meet mine and it looks like it nods. I turn to Silas, who is already studying the creature intently.

"It smells funny," I mutter, voicing my unease. It's an intricate blend of pine needles and rain-soaked earth, but underpinning it all was something that didn't belong.

"Looks like a were, but it's just a wolf," Silas replies, his brows furrowed in concentration.

But I shake my head. "Then why does it feel so… off?" The question slipped from my lips before I could stop it. The books say werewolves couldn't stay shifted when the moon isn't full. But this wolf, it holds an air of contained power, something that makes my skin tingle with recognition.

"It doesn't matter, does it?" Silas asks, brow raised. "We're only a few hours from the Lake. We need to continue."

"I suppose you're right," I murmur, tearing my gaze away from the animal to focus on our impending journey. Silas leads the way with determined strides, and I follow closely behind, the echo of the wolf's gaze burning in my mind.

The path ahead winds through the thickest part of the forest, filled with gnarled trees and tangled brambles that seem to claw at our clothes. But Silas presses on, maintaining his unyielding pace, his gaze forward. The forest seems to close in around us, the air thick with the scent of moss and earth. The path narrows, forcing us into a single file.

"Do you always move so fast?" I huff, my legs burning to keep up with his long strides.

"We can't afford to waste time," he replies without turning, his tone clipped. "The full moon is in three days now."

My chest heaves, trying to catch my breath. "We need to figure out how we're going to find my mother," I say between gasps for air. "We can't just... run blindly into danger."

"We will make a plan after we reach the Lake," he says firmly.

I know he's right, but the reminder of Amara's warnings stick with me. All that talk of tangled threads and truths and binding ties will be something to deal with. But finally, after what feels like an eternity, we emerge into a clearing and behold Prism Lake before us.

It's like a mirror made of sapphires, reflecting the surrounding landscape with a crystal clear clarity. We stop at the shore and gaze upon it.

"It's... gorgeous," I say, my voice barely above a whisper. Every detail seems to be perfectly placed in this picturesque paradise: the towering trees that provide shelter and shade, the majestic mountains to the south that create a dramatic backdrop, and the sparkling stones lining the bottom of the Lake like precious gems.

But Silas isn't focused on the Lake's beauty. He's already pulling off his shirt, revealing his pale skin that seems to glow in the light of Prism Lake. He takes a step closer to the water, his gaze fixed on me now.

"Come swim with me, Maeve," he urges.

"Excuse me?" I'm distracted... by the water, not Silas' gleaming skin.

"The finfolk are below," he says. "We'll find them with time to spare before the full moon."

Yes, the finfolk are in their unseen domain, hidden in the depths of an underwater world that presses against the underbelly of Prism Lake. Deep, deep within.

"Shouldn't we be making a plan?" I ask, my voice cracking thinking about exactly *how* deep.

"After," he says, hands closing in on the ties of his pants. "We'll appear through the water and can slip somewhere hidden to plan."

"How could I even get there, Silas?" I ask, trying to mask my alarm at getting in the water with logic. "Unless I grow gills, there's no way I'd make it."

He smiles knowingly, his silver eyes swirling with an otherworldly light. "Normally, I'd have a breathing apparatus for humans, but you won't need one. Trust me, Maeve, you can hold your breath that long."

I study him warily, fear still overtaking my rationality. *In what scenario would it be normal for a human to be expected to jump into Prism Lake and venture into the Unseen Lake?* Unless they were creatures themselves.

"I read about another way," I begin tentatively. "A portal on the center island is said to lead to Avalaruin. We can walk to the finfolk settlement from there."

A sailor left a map of Avalaruin once and Bridgit snapped it up for the library. It wasn't very detailed but at least pointed out the basics. The island at the center of the Aboveground houses a portal that opens into Avalaruin. There's a bridge to the mainland, an ominously named Forest of

Shadows, and then an entrance to the underwater finfolk settlement through a nearby cave.

Silas' expression turns grave. "The portal is not safe, Maeve. There are worse things than finfolk living in Avalaruin. It's unpredictable and dangerous. Trust me when I say diving is our best option."

I glance back at the tranquil surface of Prism Lake, trying to imagine swimming through it. As beautiful and clear as it is, the thought still makes me nauseous. "I'm willing to risk it."

He frowns. "I—"

"This is my fire," I remind him again. "Isn't there a boat or something? *Surely* that's a faster alternative than you needing to save me from drowning every few seconds because I seize up from fear." Boats are said to be stationed at various points along the lake, placed there by fae to allow for easy travel for creatures between the Aboveground and Avalaruin worlds.

"Unless the books are wrong," I continue, a question in my tone.

"Not about that," he says begrudgingly.

"And... there's no rule or law that I can't take the boat?"

With a sigh, he looks to the sky, the sun high above us. I know he's thinking of the full moon coming. "... Not that I can think of," he admits.

Frustration flickers across his face before he nods slowly. "Fine," he concedes. "We'll go along the shore a bit until we reach one of those boats that will take us to the center island. *Without* delay," he adds, scowling at me.

Following his lead, we walk along the edge of Prism Lake, the water lapping gently against the pebbled shore. But no matter how calm it looks, the water in that rippling surface tightens its grip on my heart.

Soon enough, we find the boats bobbing along the shoreline, each uniquely crafted, decorated with intricate carvings and vibrant colors. Silas picks a boat painted a brilliant purple with a dragon's head carved into the prow, its eyes seeming to follow us as we approach.

As we reach the edge of the water, I hesitate, staring at the small vessel. The water is inviting, but it's what lies beneath that causes me fear.

Silas steps into the boat first and extends a hand towards me. "Come on, Maeve."

I remind myself I'm 'New Maeve,' who frees selkies and bargains with seers. With a deep breath, I take his hand and step into the boat beside him. The wood creaks under our weight as we push off from the shore. I sit with my knees hugged tight to my chest as we glide towards the center island, the water glass-like as we float.

"Nearly halfway," he says minutes later in a low voice, breaking the silence.

"Feels like forever," I whisper, each word a tremble. I can't look over the side of the boat.

"Keep your eyes on the island and you'll be fine," Silas instructs, his voice distant and detached.

Yet it's difficult for me to focus on anything but my own anxieties as we continue our journey across Prism Lake towards the unknown depths of the finfolk domain.

That's when they come. A haunting melody drifts through the air, carried on a gentle breeze that stirs my hair. Heads breach the surface. Their hair floats like seaweed, their eyes black voids, and their voices fill the air with an enchanting song. Sirens. They circle our boat, their faces ethereal and too beautiful to be real. Suddenly, I'm no longer fearful of what lies *beneath* those serene waters.

"I've heard about them," I whisper, watching them with awe. Mama's stories about the sirens were my second favorite, after the selkies. "They're attracted to magical creatures."

And now they're attracted to us, their hypnotic song tugging at my senses.

But Silas' attention is focused solely on the sirens, his grip tightening on the wooden seat as they draw closer. One of them leans against the side of the boat, her lips painted in a dark red smirk.

"Beautiful traveler," she purrs, her voice a bewitching melody that curls around me. "Your essence is... intriguing. I would not expect to find you in one of these boats."

"Leave us be," Silas demands, his voice cutting through the siren's enchanting words.

Another siren appears beside the first, her voice like molten honey. "Will you join us in the water?" She reaches out a hand towards me, the water parting around her pale skin. "We'll swim together in the shallows."

Silas' jaw clenches. "Enough," he growls, never taking his eyes off the creatures. "We have no business with you."

The first siren's lips twist into a semblance of a smile, but it doesn't reach her eyes. They remain cold, like the depths they called home. "We don't answer to you, creature."

"Now, listen here—" My voice cracks, but he's already moving, positioning himself between me and the emerging figures.

The boat rocks with his sudden movement, and before I can react, the sirens' demeanor changes. A low hiss escapes their lips, their eyes narrowing in anger at Silas' interference.

"Stay down, Maeve," he snaps, just as more heads pop up around us. Their beauty is terrible, mesmerizing, but their gazes are fixed on Silas with an intensity that turns my blood cold.

One lunges, sleek and swift, her song a screech that claws at the air. Tails whip out of the water, striking the sides of the boat with resounding cracks. The boat rocks violently under the force of their powerful tails, threatening to capsize at any moment. I clutch onto the edges in a desperate attempt to steady myself, my heart pounding in my chest as fear clenches its icy grip around me. I can't end up in the water.

"She's mine," someone snarls, but I can't tell who, the cacophony of the sirens' melodies and crashing waves blocking it out.

Their voices rise in a crescendo of anger and desire, Silas, the sirens, anyone. The boat pitches under the force of the fight; I lose my balance. A scream tears from my throat as I topple overboard, plunging into the clear waters of Prism Lake.

"Silas!" The name bursts from me in a bubble, the surface just beyond reach. Panic claws at my chest, a wild thing with sharp teeth. My limbs fail, I can't tell which way is up, but the lake is relentless, dragging me deeper.

Gone are the sirens, gone is the boat, gone is Silas. Only water—a suffocating, endless blue—that swallows me whole.

Then silence. A hush falls over my frantic thoughts, the struggle easing as if a spell had been cast. The water is no longer an enemy but a cradle, rocking me gently into the depths.

I drift, caught between worlds, and my eyes flutter closed...

...only to open upon a dreamscape of ethereal beauty. A cavern beneath the waves, its walls aglow with luminescence, cradling creatures of legend: kelpies, werewolves, nagas, finfolk. Seals—or are they selkies?—flit along the currents, their sleek forms twirling with a grace that defies reality. They're everything Mama said: smooth, opalescent fur that glimmers in the underwater light, eyes that swirl like shimmering scales. One seal approaches, her eyes reflecting the myriad colors of the ocean. They're a swirling vortex, just like Silas', just like Mama's. Just like mine.

She whispers in a language older than time, her voice the tide's lullaby, "Trust the water, as it trusts you."

Her touch is soft, a brush against my cheek that feels like coming home. The seals swirl around us, their movements painting the water with streaks of silver and gold.

"Embrace your nature," she urges, her form blurring, shifting—human one moment, seal the next. "Use your fire. Use your teeth."

Chapter 7

A selkie's ability to transform between seal and human forms hinges on their skin, which they must shed in order to walk on land. If a human, driven by desire or love, takes or hides a selkie's seal skin, they effectively imprison the selkie in human form and sever their connection to the sea. This act of theft traps the selkie in a world where they do not fully belong, leading to a poignant struggle between their

> *longing for the ocean and the human's attempts to keep them captive. This often results in a life of unfulfilled yearning and sorrow.*
>
> -Excerpt from Beneath the Surface: Unveiling the Mysteries of Selkies and Finfolk.

Gasping, sputtering, the world rushes back in a violent tide. Silas' hands are on me, pressing rhythmically against my chest as he breathes life back into my lungs. My eyes fluttered open to an overcast sky, the edges of my vision blurred and undulating like the water that had tried to claim me.

"Breathe, Maeve," he urges between compressions, his voice a desperate command.

Then, more air. Sweet, precious air fills me, burning its way down my throat as I cough out the Lake's remnants.

I lie there, gasping and trembling, the echo of the underwater dream still lingering at the edges of my mind. Silas' face hovers above me, a blend of relief and worry etched into his features before he wipes the emotions away. His hands are warm on my skin and he sparkles like a diamond in the light. He must have gone into the water for me.

Struggling to sit up, I push myself onto shaky elbows, my gaze meeting his. The selkies, the sirens, the fall into the lake, the... dream (*was it a dream?*)—it all feels like a maelstrom that leaves me dizzy and disoriented.

"Are you okay?" Silas' voice cuts through the fog in my mind, pulling me back to reality. Even with his blank mask on now, his expression has an intensity that matches the roiling within me.

I nod weakly, still catching my breath. "Are we... are we there yet?" I ask.

"Not quite," Silas replies, helping me sit up. His hand is steady on my shoulder, grounding. "The portal is close. We can make it."

I turn back to the Lake, which looks placid and gentle again. The sunlight reflecting off the surface seems to wink at me. *Trust the water*, the dream had said. *Did that mean I should return to its embrace?* Mama *is* in there. *Is that how I find her?*

I shiver, and not from the damp, the high sun beating down on me overhead. Fear still finds me, no matter how kind the water was to me this time.

"Can you stand?" Silas' brow creases with concern, a stark contrast to the firm set of his jaw.

I nod, more out of stubbornness than any real confidence in my ability. With his help, I rise unsteadily to my feet, my legs trembling beneath me. The island is both minuscule and vast, a solitary refuge amidst the expanse of Prism Lake.

"Good," Silas says, his gaze scanning our surroundings. "We need to keep moving."

His hand moves to his side, where the fabric of his shirt is torn and stained with blood. I follow his gesture, my breath catching as I see the gash marring his skin.

I gasp. "Gods, you're hurt!"

Silas brushes off my concern with a tight-lipped smile. "It's nothing," he murmurs. "Are you ready?"

"Let me help," I insist, reaching out tentatively towards his wound.

He flinches slightly at my touch, his eyes fixed inward on the island. "It's nothing, I said," he says through gritted teeth. "Let's go. Now."

The sight of his blood brings forth the gravity of what had just happened. The weight of it all seems to drag me down, making it hard to even stand.

"I need a minute," I breathe. "We've been going nonstop since leaving the village. I know the moon is coming in a few days, but it can let us sit for a minute."

Silas' jaw tightens as he looks towards the water. "We took a break last night," he bites out. "That already delayed us."

"Sleeping isn't a break," I say, heaving out a breath. I close my eyes, trying to shake off being the dream and peril I haven't recovered from. "You're hurt," I say pointedly. "I almost died."

"You didn't almost die," Silas tries to interrupt, but I don't let him.

"If ever we were going to take a break," I say, my voice rising, "it would be now."

My gaze drifts up to meet his as a numbness settles over me. Why *did* the sirens react to him with such venom? What secrets does his past hold that could unsettle creatures of the deep? This must be the truth Amara mentioned, whatever it may be. But why did they want *me*, a human with no magic to speak of?

My voice is quiet as I ask, "What in the hells even happened out there, Silas?"

Any hesitation he had at stopping dies with the question. His expression darkens, a flicker of something unspoken crossing his eyes before he masks it with a steely resolve. "You drew the sirens to us, Maeve. Engaging with them was reckless.

That's what happened. And now you need to get up before you do something else."

The numb confusion I felt fades with the flash of irritation. "Reckless?" I repeat, the word sharp on my tongue.

"We can argue about this later," Silas insists. "Right now, we need to reach the portal before anything else goes wrong." He scowls down at me. "Before you do anything else wrong."

"Me? You were the one who insisted on coming here, the one who brought me into this mess in the first place!"

A flicker of hurt crosses his face before his features harden once more. "We're doing this for *you*, remember," he retorts. "I... could have gone on my own."

I glare at him, frustration bubbling up within me. "Then go. I'll find the finfolk on my own."

Silas' jaw tightens, his gaze flickering over my face before it settles into a blank mask. "No. I made you a promise to take you to the finfolk."

"I won't be rushed by you," I declare, my tone unwavering. "Not until you tell me what actually happened back there with the sirens," I demand. My voice falters slightly as I gesture towards the lake, my mind still replaying the memory of their menacing tails and sharp teeth. "And don't you *dare* blame me."

Silas' eyes narrow, his jaw tensing as he regards me with a mix of exasperation and guardedness. "Sirens and selkies... they don't always live... harmoniously. There's an ancient feud between our kinds that goes back centuries."

I frown, the explanation ringing hollow in my ears. "But I thought they were friends, that they both shared the waters."

He hesitates, his gaze flickering away for a beat before meeting mine. "Remember that books aren't always true, Maeve. Beneath the surface, alliances can shift like the tides."

An uneasy feeling settles in the pit of my stomach, mingling with the remnants of fear and confusion from the water's depths. A book hadn't taught me that. Mama did. She had always painted a picture of peaceful coexistence and camaraderie beneath the waves.

But why would she know more than Silas? the rational part of me asks. *She wouldn't.*

I take a deep breath, the tang of salt on my tongue and push it all—the question, the sirens, the dream—aside. "What time is it in Avalaruin?" He raises his brows and I repeat the question.

He glances up at the sky. It's already well on its way towards dusk here. "The morning," he responds.

Hope rises. If it's already morning here, then surely the finfolk will be awake and busy with their daily tasks. "I may not have infiltrated many strongholds before, but when everyone is scurrying around likely isn't the best time, is it?"

His shoulders slump and I know I've won. At least for now.

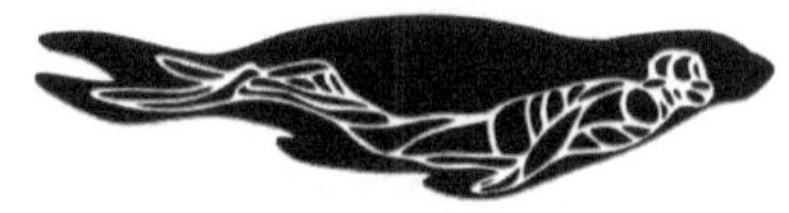

The sky bleeds orange and lavender, and the lake mirrors the colors like a still, polished glass. We agreed to wait on the island until closer to sunset in Avalaruin before infiltrating, when it would be not quite dawn here. Now I sit on the gritty sand, trying to sort through the tangle of my thoughts. The sirens, the water, the dreams, my mother—it all churns inside me, restless and unresolved.

Silas paces a short distance away, his shadow stretching long in the fading light. He has said little since our argument earlier, but his frustration hangs in the air, thick and oppressive.

I want to be angry with him. Truly, I do. He rushed me, he dismissed my questions, and he somehow made me feel like a fool for almost drowning. But now, seeing him so tightly wound, I can only feel tired.

"We could use a plan," I say finally, breaking the silence.

He stops in his tracks, turning to face me with a weary expression. "The grand infiltration," he says with a hint of unnecessary sarcasm. "We have a plan."

I raise my brows. "Do we?"

His jaw tightens, but he doesn't argue. Instead, he sits down on the sand beside me, his movements stiff and reluctant. He keeps a careful distance, as if being too close might spark another fight. "We slip in unnoticed, find your mother, and slip out. Simple." His attempt at nonchalance is as transparent as water.

I draw my knees up, wrapping my arms around them. "Simple," I echo, but my mind races with the complexities, the dangers.

There's a ferocity brewing within me, a tempest wanting to break free, if only I let it. For a moment, I indulge the thought of unleashing it upon the finfolk settlement, letting fire consume wood and stone until nothing remains but cinders dancing on the tide. But I remember what Silas said: the books could have it wrong. Maybe they're not all bad actors.

"You said unnoticed," I press, needing details to tether the fury. "How do we manage that?"

"Since we're not swimming in, we take the cave passage. There's only one guarded entrance and we can certainly manage that," he says, rubbing a hand across his face. "It isn't exactly a fortress. There are blind spots, patrols with gaps long enough to slip through if you know where to look."

"And the dungeons?"

"Underground, mostly," he says. "But I know the layout."

I let out a breath, feeling some of the tension leave my body. "Where will your pelt be?"

"We'll get it," he says, not answering. There's something hollow in his voice, as if the words are more for my benefit than his own.

"We should plan that, too," I tell him. After all, this part of our journey is all about me and finding my mother, but the full moon looms.

"It's fine," he says, but there's a tremor in his voice. "It will all work out."

He stares out at the lake, his shoulders hunched like he carries the weight of the world on his back. For all his sharpness, he looks... tired. Worn thin in a way I've not noticed before.

"What's it like?" I ask, shifting topics. "Living like a selkie?"

He pauses, clearly surprised by the question. "It's... life," he starts, then falters, choosing his words with care. "The sea is home. It's where you belong, where every current sings of ancient tales and the depth embraces you like a long-lost lover. There can be nowhere else for a... a selkie."

His description sounds genuine, wistful even, but something doesn't sit right, like a puzzle piece forced into the wrong space. "Do you... miss it?" I ask.

"It's all I know," he whispers, almost too quiet to catch. There's a longing there, but it's edged with guilt, like a knife honed on regret.

"There are other options," I say, the words slipping out before I can stop them. I never took that step, leaving my village, until I had the chance of Mama with me. That might be what Silas needs, someone to give him the offer to start over and not be alone.

"Other options?" Silas repeats, turning his gaze from the hill to me.

I take a deep breath. "I know you were concerned about that selkie ritual. And I thought—I mean... once we find my mother and get your pelt back, we could all start a new life. Together."

"I never... considered that," Silas finally says, his voice rough with emotion. "I always thought... this was all there was for me. This life, but apart."

"There's always a choice, Silas," I say softly. "You don't have to be bound by fate or tradition. We can forge our own path together, write our own story. You deserve a chance at a different kind of life."

He speaks again, his voice low and rough. "You don't understand what it's like to belong to something so completely and still feel... trapped."

I watch him carefully, trying to piece together the layers of meaning behind his words. "No," I admit, "I don't. But I understand what it's like to be trapped without belonging at all. You just need to try."

He exhales sharply, a sound that could almost be a laugh if it weren't so bitter. "You make it sound so easy."

"I didn't say it was easy," I counter, my chin lifting slightly. "I said it was possible." If I didn't think the same, if there wasn't a chance for me, I may not have left my cottage.

He studies me in the dimming light, his silver eyes swirling with something I can't quite name. It's not anger or frustration this time. It's something deeper, something hesitant and vulnerable

The moment stretches, and my cheeks heat under his gaze. I look away, focusing on the lake instead. "I'm just saying it's worth thinking about," I mumble.

"Maeve," he breathes, and the sound of my name in his voice makes my heart skip. "You're..." He stops himself, his lips pressing into a thin line as if he's said too much already. He shakes his head slightly, a rueful smile ghosting across his face. "Never mind."

I glance at him, startled by the shift in his expression. There's something in his eyes that feels almost... tender. It's fleeting, gone as quickly as it appeared, but it lingers between us like the faint scent of salt and brine.

"What?" I press, my curiosity piqued despite myself.

He drags a hand through his hair, his fingers catching briefly in the damp strands. The silence stretches between us again, but it doesn't feel oppressive this time. It feels like the beginning of something unspoken.

"I am sorry about the sirens, and our argument," he finally says.

"It's... fine," I tell him. "We're still in this together, squabbles and all."

His expression softens again, almost imperceptibly, but I catch it like a glimmer of sunlight on the water. "Together."

Chapter 8

Throughout history, the relationship between selkies and finfolk has been one marked by conflict, stemming from their divergent lifestyles and competing interests. One of the most well-documented conflicts between selkies and finfolk revolves around territorial disputes in coastal areas. Selkies often prefer shallow, protected waters and rocky shorelines for their transformations and gatherings. Finfolk, on the other hand, inhabit deeper waters and underwater realms but frequently encroach upon selkie territories during their forays into shallower regions. Cultural differences further exacerbate the tension. Selkies are generally more inclined toward peaceful interactions and value their connection to both the human and marine worlds. Their dual existence allows them to appreciate the beauty and tranquility of both realms, fostering a culture of balance and harmony. In contrast, finfolk are often more insular and aggressive, driven by a desire to dominate and control.

-Excerpt from Beneath the Surface: Unveiling the Mysteries of Selkies and Finfolk.

The portal spits us out into Avalaruin, a dark and foreboding world that's a twisted version of the island we just left. The trees here are thin and spindly, their branches reaching out like skeletal hands. Where it was pre-dawn in the Aboveground, it's dusk here. In front of us lies Unseen Lake, its waters almost black under the eerie moonlight and shrouded by a thick layer of mist.

I want to ask Silas if he knows whether the rest of Avalaruin looks this way or if there are pockets of magic and beauty hidden deeper within like the books say. But his warning about the dangers here keeps me quiet, my fear as thick as the underbrush that tangles itself around the worn path leading to the bridge over Unseen Lake.

"Watch your step," Silas says, his voice barely carrying over the creaking of the bridge beneath our feet. It sways with every gust, planks groaning as if in pain, threatening to pitch us into the abyss below. I keep my eyes fixed ahead, away from the drop. Dream or no dream, this is the water that will give me nightmares.

I awoke this morning to find the energy between Silas and me... different. Something had softened overnight. He held my gaze a little longer when I asked about the plan and portal, his responses measured instead of sharp. And when he reached out to help me with the supplies, his hand brushed mine, his first time reaching for me instead of the reverse. But any sense of comfort it might have offered is smothered by the ever-present knot of fear in my chest. All I can focus on is the bridge beneath my feet and the water below, waiting for the moment it all gives way.

"Think I can handle a bridge, thank you," I say, my nerves frayed.

Silas hums, a low sound that's somehow more infuriating than words. "Like you handled the boat?"

I whip my head towards him, shooting him a glare sharp enough to cut. "The boat was your fault."

"Come on," he says, his voice softer now, steadying. "We're almost across. I won't let you fall, Maeve."

The words are simple, but they carry a quiet certainty that anchors me, even as the wind tries to pull me off balance. I swallow hard, my focus returning to the path ahead.

"You'd better not," I murmur, half to myself.

Behind me, I hear him chuckle softly. "I didn't let you drown, did I?"

I grit my teeth, refusing to rise to the bait this time. But a small, unwanted smile tugs at the corners of my lips as I take the next step forward.

A sudden gust of wind sweeps through the trees, making the bridge groan even louder under our weight. A piece of rotten wood gives way beneath my foot, and I lurch forward. Panic seizes me as the abyss yawns below, ready to swallow me whole. But before I can plummet into the murky depths of Unseen Lake, powerful arms wrap around me, pulling me back from the edge.

"Careful," Silas murmurs, his voice softer now, devoid of its earlier teasing.

"Don't," I tell him, embarrassment creeping up my cheeks. *Don't remind me of what I said a minute ago. Don't let go.*

His grip tightens on my hand and he leads us towards the mainland. "I've done nothing," he says. There's a lightness to his voice but he can't mask the tremble. *Is he worried about me?*

We finally reach the end of the bridge and Silas drops my hand just as one of those twisted trees comes to life. It looms over us, a massive mass of twisted bark and roots that seem to claw at the sky. Its bright red eyes glare at us with a cold intelligence as it begins to move, the ground shaking with each deliberate step towards us.

For a minute, I imagine turning and running, the bridge offering a treacherous escape. But then I remember the way it swayed, the creaks and groans, and I know it wouldn't hold against the wrath of this behemoth if it chases us.

Silas edges closer to me, his arm brushing against mine in a show of solidarity. "Don't make any sudden moves," he whispers urgently, his confident demeanor replaced by a cautious fear. "That's a holly treeman and it will kill you."

I don't need the warning. The creature towers over us, its presence demanding respect—or fear, which it seems more than happy to instill. I can taste the threat in the air, heavy and cloying, a prelude to violence I'm ill-prepared to face.

"Any ideas?" I ask, trying to keep my voice steady despite the pounding of my heart. "Or are charming forest monsters as difficult for you as sirens?"

"Let me think," Silas hisses, though there's no bite in his words.

He could have reminded me that it was my fault we took the portal rather than swimming to the finfolk domain, that I took us this way. But he doesn't.

With that thought churning in my stomach, I swallow hard when Silas' eyes dart from the creature to me, a plan sparking behind his gaze.

"Listen," he whispers. "We must improvise. Remember how your family thought I was a finfolk?" I nod and he continues, "Well, maybe this creature will believe the same."

My brows knit together. "How?"

"A shapeshifter's a shapeshifter, right? Close enough for our friend here." He jerks his head toward the monster. "We need to sell it a story. We are... entwined, let's say. You'll be my conquest."

"Conquest?" The word tastes bitter, but panic is a potent motivator. "Like captured?"

"Exactly." His eyes hold mine, pleading for co-operation. "It's crucial. It might think twice about attacking if it believes I've claimed you. As a wife," he's quick to add, as if to ease any discomfort. "Not a slave. Never that."

I can think of no better plan but this lie. I put us on this path, so if anything happens to me, it will be on my head. Assuming I get to keep it.

"Fine," I spit out, hating every syllable. Not because a connection to him is unwelcome, but because it would be forced. I wonder if Mama ever got the choice. "But only because I prefer not be-ing tree fodder."

"Right." Silas steps closer, weaving his fingers through mine. His hand is warm, solid. "Remem-ber, you're a hostage I've tricked into falling madly in love with me and I'm taking you as my wife. Let's make it convincing."

My heart races, whether from fear or the forced intimacy of a man I secretly find attractive, I can't tell. But survival trumps all, and so I lean into him, hoping my face tells the story he needs it to.

"Come on," he murmurs, pulling me gently. "Let's charm ourselves a monster."

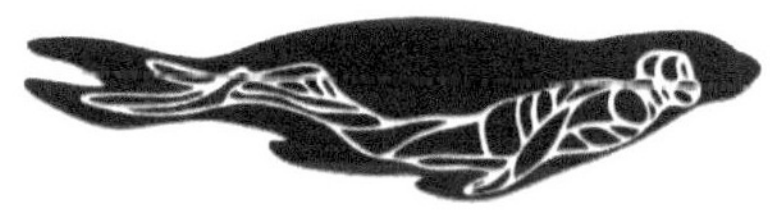

The bridge creaks beneath our feet, its protest lost in the swirl of mist that clung to the island's edge. We step onto solid ground, but relief is a stranger here.

"Visitors," the tree monster rumbles in a voice that resembles a symphony of snapping branches and rustling leaves. Its eyes gleam with hunger as it towers over us, its bark-encrusted limbs weaving an intimidating canopy. A thin branch whips towards my face in a sharp caress.

Silas stiffens beside me, his grip on my hand tightening. He emits a low growl that surprises me with its ferocity. His eyes glint with violence, and his stance exudes a power I have never seen before. It's as if he has shed his human-selkie skin to reveal a false finfolk form below.

"She's mine," he snarls at the creature.

The tree monster recoils slightly, its branches rustling in surprise. "Ah, a finfolk," it rumbles, its voice now tinged with a mixture of respect and wariness. "I should have known by the scent you carry." It leans closer, its breath reeking of decay. "A fine prize. Will you share her warmth or dine alone?"

"Neither," he spits back. I can almost believe the venom in his words. Almost. "I'm not sharing, and I'm certainly not eating. At least, not outside the bedroom." His fingers dig into mine, a silent plea for me to play along.

The creature's gaze shifts between us, as if searching for the truth. "You plan to wed her? Make her yours in ways other than servitude? You're nearly late for the ceremony."

Silas squeezes my hand, a silent signal that must say both 'hold on' and 'be ready.' I force a smile, tilting my head to rest against Silas' arm. *Let it believe the lie. Let it believe I am deceived and willing to serve my finfolk husband.* My heart hammers, a wild thing caged within my ribs. Silas' scent—salty and stormy—fills my senses and for a moment, I sway towards him not out of pretense but out of actual interest.

"She does, I do," Silas growls.

The creature's eyes flicker with a curiosity, though I can't tell if it senses the falsehood in our charade. "Been a long time since I've seen a finborn take a spouse without chains. This one *seems* to like you," the tree monster rumbles finally, a tangle of roots shifting beneath us as if to emphasize its point. More branches withdraw from its trunk and try to slither up my arm.

Silas bats them away, stepping between me and the creature. "Touch what's mine again, and you'll feel the wrath of the sea itself," he warns, his voice low and dangerous.

It retreats a foot, its branches drooping in submission. "Apologies, finborn. I meant no disrespect. I was simply confused. I've been tricked lately."

"Not all of us must snatch our humans," Silas says. He runs his own finger down my cheek. "There are other ways."

My heart thuds in my chest. It's fake, it's all an act, but the intensity of his gaze and the heat radiating from his body leave me dizzy and breathless. I hold my breath, trying to remember this is all a game.

"Give this old tree a glimpse of something it hasn't seen up close in centuries," the creature says slyly.

Silas maintains a steady gaze on me as he speaks, his voice firm and unwavering. "You are owed nothing from us."

The tree monster lets out a deep, rumbling chuckle that shakes the ground beneath us. Its branches sway gently. "Fair enough," it concedes, its eyes fixed on us with a gleam of mischief. "I simply thought a couple in love would have no reason to deny a demonstration of their love."

Silas tenses beside me, his jaw clenching. I can think of a dozen reasons why a real 'couple in love' wouldn't want to perform for an audience. But no matter the tree monster's genial attitude now, it could turn on us like a shark in the shallows.

Without speaking, without even needing to vocalize our next move, we both understand what is needed to convince this ancient being.

Silas steps closer, his hand gently cupping my cheek as he stares into my eyes. The touch sends shivers down my spine, not from fear but inappropriate interest, that good discomfort being near him makes me feel. His own expression looks less pained than I'd expect and I let that realization push me forward. Closing the distance between us, I lift my chin defiantly, step on my tiptoes to reach his tall form, and press my lips against his, my arms wrapping around his neck. And the world seems to fade away.

The kiss deepens, his fingers tangle in my hair, and I'm a ship caught in a tempest, torn between the desire to surrender and the need to stay afloat. Soon, too soon, too long...we pull away from each other.

I meet Silas' gaze, noticing how his swirling eyes have softened. I wonder if mine are doing the same.

The tree monster claps its branches together loudly, jolting us back to attention. "Very good," it says with a rustling sound that sounds almost like laughter. "Then I won't keep you from the lunar ceremony any longer. But heed my warning: the woods have eyes, finborn."

Silas gives a curt nod in response. "We understand the dangers," he replies. "I will not be idle."

"Ah, but are you sure?" The creature's bark twists into what might have been a smirk. "Remember, trading flesh is forbidden. Seduction or no. And that includes humans... and their kin. What say you complete the ritual and your girl is taken from you?"

My pulse quickens, all confusing thoughts from the kiss vanishing into the mist behind us. *Trading? What did this have to do with me?*

"That won't happen," Silas says, but the determination in his voice fades, as he asks, "Forbidden since when?"

"Since the treaty," the monster says, looming closer. "You must know all beings of magic are bound by it. Fae, vampires, werewolves, any creature by any human... No exceptions."

I watch Silas carefully, trying to decipher his thoughts through our facade. He had known about finfolk stealing humans, but whatever this is? This seems new to him.

"That's... unexpected," Silas mutters, almost to himself. His hand tightens around mine and I don't know what's running through his head. "No exceptions at all?" he asks, sounding uninterested.

"My mistake," the creature says, and Silas' neck nearly cracks with the speed he looks up at it. "I'd forgotten. Half-humans are exempt from the law."

It turns its gnarled face towards me with a chilling leer. "Take care, girl. Your kind is so... soft. One squeeze and it's over."

Silas' eyes widen imperceptibly and he shutters that fearsome finfolk mask back over his face. "I take care of what's mine," he growls. "Thank you, comrade."

"Indeed." The creature's gaze lingers on me. "Good marriage to you both."

The monstrous form of the treeman recedes into the forest, swallowed by the shadows and the whispering leaves.

"Well, that went better than expected," he murmurs, a hint of relief in his voice. He lets out a heavy breath, his shoulders relaxing slightly, though his hold on me doesn't loosen. His eyes flick to me, the corners of his mouth twitching into a faint smirk. "About the kiss—"

My cheeks heat against my will. "We can talk about that later. There are more important things to talk about. Like human *trading*?"

He's silent for a moment, his gaze fixed on my face, but I can't read his expression. "Long ago," he finally says, his tone low, "the creatures of magic realized humans were too... fragile for our world. Too unexceptional. So, we made a pact—a treaty—to protect them, to keep the balance."

"Protect them from what?" I press, unease curling in my gut.

"From us," he admits, and there's something in his voice—a hint of guilt—that sets my teeth on edge. "From becoming pawns in our conflicts or curiosities in our collections."

"Did selkies—" I start to ask before cutting myself off. No, selkies were stolen by humans, not the other way around. But then another thought curls through my mind. "Since when has this treaty been in place?"

"Longer than my life," he says. "At least a few hundred years." His eyes narrow slightly as he studies me. "None of you even live close to that long, do you?"

But I'm not listening to his musings—not when my own thoughts are crashing over me like waves. A few hundred years. The words echo in my mind like a curse. The memory of my mother—her smile, her laughter—flashes before my eyes. Twenty years ago, the finfolk took her. They stole her. They violated this treaty.

A surge of anger rises in my chest, hot and consuming. "Then they broke it," I spit. "The finfolk took my mother—violated the treaty! And no one did anything? No one cared?!"

Silas' face tightens, his expression flickering between regret and something more pained. "It's... it's not—" he says, but I cut him off.

"Shouldn't you be more upset?" I ask sharply, bitterness coating every word.

The sirens that tried to lure me into the water, the finfolk who stole my mother, the tree creature that wanted to devour me—no one cares. I'm prey in Avalaruin and in the Aboveground, to the creatures and to men like my father. My heart pounds, a drumbeat of fear and fury, each step an echo of the anger seething inside me. A betrayal twenty years deep claws at my insides, demanding vengeance. "You're so interested in legalities, you'd think you'd be as troubled as I am at the violation."

"I am troubled by it," he says, not meeting my eyes. "It's illegal."

"It's barbaric," I snap, my voice trembling with a mix of emotions, anger, hurt, and a new fear that Silas may not be the ally I desperately need in this strange and treacherous world. The weight of betrayal, both recent and long-standing, bears down on me. "You'd think the selkies would care, since they're stolen so often by humans."

"I do care, Maeve," he says, finally turning to face me, his expression pained. He wets his lips, the skin shiny. "Maybe... maybe this isn't the right way. Maybe we leave, look into the treaty more, find another way." His hand loosens on mine as if the weight of my anger is too much to bear. "Find another way to start over, like you said. Without the risk of entering the... the underwater finfolk domain."

For a moment, his words linger in the air between us, tempting, even kind, as though he's finally acknowledging my fear without teasing. But I can't accept them. Not now.

"No," I say firmly. "We don't need a loophole, Silas." My voice hardens, my resolve steady. "Every moment spent here is another she's suffering. We need to get to the finfolk."

Silas opens his mouth, whether to argue or placate me, I'm not sure, but I cut him off before he can speak.

"If you're not with me, I'll find her myself," I declare, my voice ringing with a newfound determination that even surprised me. "I don't need your laws or your loopholes. I just need answers. Are you coming with me or not?"

For a long moment, Silas doesn't move. His quicksilver eyes shift, the turmoil in them almost too much to bear. Finally, he nods and gestures toward the dark path ahead.

We walk in silence, but this time, something is different. His steps are slower, more deliberate, as though he's no longer rushing toward his pelt, towards my mother. But it doesn't matter what he intends to do. Because now, I'm leading the way.

Chapter 9

Identifying selkies and finfolk in their human forms can be challenging due to their remarkable ability to blend in with humans. However, keen observers may notice subtle differences that set these creatures apart. One of the most telling characteristics of finfolk is the texture of their skin, particularly after they have been in contact with water. Finfolk retain a scaly appearance on

> *their skin even after they emerge from the water, giving away their true nature. This scalelike pattern can range from barely noticeable to prominent, depending on the age and health of the finfolk.*
>
> -Excerpt from Beneath the Surface: Unveiling the Mysteries of Selkies and Finfolk.

Plan be damned, my fury will likely light the finfolk stronghold on fire. If only they were as fearful of flames as Silas' species is. Still, my flint and firestriker are shoved into my shoes. Just in case.

Dropping our bags at the entrance, we slip into the cave like a silent ripple, our shadows blending seamlessly with the darkness. Jagged stalactites hang from the ceiling, dripping with moisture, while stalagmites rise from the ground like ancient, weathered pillars. It would be beautiful if it wasn't the entrance to a cavern of monsters.

We navigate the maze of glowing tunnels, each one filled with crystal clear water and bioluminescent plants that cast a soft, ethereal glow along the walls. The path is a labyrinth of forks and dead ends that trails deep into the earth. Silas trudges behind me, gesturing listlessly towards which direction to take. But every step forward only adds to my determination; we won't be sneaking in and out unnoticed. We'll be making waves.

And Silas... he's still different, affected by our exchange about human trading. His expression is harder to read than ever, his usual confidence dimmed by something quieter—something that feels almost like doubt. His shoulders slump, and his movements lack their usual purpose. It's as though the weight of something unseen drags him down with every step.

"Silas?" My voice cuts through the silence as I reach for his hand. "Can you play finfolk again? When we get there, like you did with the treeman. And we can figure out our next steps once we're inside."

"Fine." His response is clipped, and I can almost taste the copper tang of fear in his voice.

The tunnel walls seem to close in, damp and alive with whispered echoes of water dripping from unseen cracks. Every fork in the path feels like a choice that leads to ruin—mine or the finfolk's,

I can't yet tell. My pulse pounds in my ears as I imagine what's waiting for us deeper inside.

Then, Silas tugs on my hand, stopping me before we take another turn. "Maeve," he says softly, his voice laced with something I can't quite place.

I turn back towards him. The reflection of the water distorts his features, making it hard to gauge his expression, but his trembling hand in mine is unmistakable. "What's wrong? Are you afraid?" My fingers tighten around his.

"Yes." The word comes out like an exhalation, soft and raw.

For a moment, the admission startles me. Silas has been the steady one, the one with the answers—even when they were ones I didn't want to hear or seemed too glib. To see him falter now feels like the waves changing directions.

I grasp his hands tighter, grounding us both. "Look, before we get there, I just want to say... thank you." My voice softens, and I force myself to meet his gaze, even as emotion threatens to overwhelm me. "The last few days have been... emotional," I say, skirting around our missteps, misunderstandings, and near-death experiences. "And we haven't always seen eye to eye, but it's been..." I hesitate, searching for the right word. "It's been nice having you with me."

Silas' expression softens at my words, his eyes lingering on mine as a faint smile tugs at his lips. In that moment, he looks less troubled than he has since revealing the dark truth about human trading.

Guided by that look, I wrap my arms around him in a tight embrace. His body tenses briefly, as if he's unsure how to respond, but then his arms come up, circling me with an unexpected gentleness. He holds me like I'm something fragile, something worth protecting.

"When we succeed, when we find my mother and your pelt," I whisper into his chest, "remember my offer. We can start over, belong somewhere together."

Silas gently places a hand on my shoulder and pulls back slightly. His eyes search mine, a mixture of longing and sadness.

"Silas, what is it?" My voice is a whisper, barely louder than the soft drip of water echoing through the cavern.

"I..." He hesitates, his words hanging in the air like a sandcastle bracing against a sharp tide. "I don't..."

Before he can drag out whatever he wants to say, the sound of growling reaches us from around the last corner. We spring apart, both looking for someone, or something, for the source of the noise. My heart leaps towards my throat. It means we're almost there.

With determination overtaking my fear, I step ahead and yank Silas along with me. His hesitation feels heavy, but I'm too focused on reaching our goal to stop now.

"Maeve, wait—" he says, but I don't let him stop us. We can't afford any more delays.

"Come on!" I urge, not looking back. "We're nearly there."

One final turn and we emerge into a vast cavern, its walls lined with a tall archway that must lead to the domain of the finfolk. Finfolk guards circle like sharks, carrying glimmering tridents, poised and ready to attack. Half of them look humanoid, their skin shimmering like scales that seem to shift and change in the low light of the cavern. They're all different shades: pale as moonlight, like Silas, deep ebony, golden, and ruddy pink. The non-humanoids still stand like humans, but with fishlike faces with gaping mouths and bulbous eyes. Most of them have long lustrous hair, pulled back into intricate braids and adorned with pearls and shells. But all of them, every single one, have swirling eyes that look like a maelstrom. A surge of panic rises, for a moment wondering why in the hells I was rushing to them, but Silas' hand is steady in mine—a lifeline amidst the storm.

"Stay close," he whispers, squeezing my fingers before letting go. It's showtime.

Silas squares his shoulders, lifts his chin, and steps forward. "Evening, lads," he calls out, his voice echoing off the stone. The guards snarl, but Silas meets their rage head on.

"I need passage," Silas says smoothly. "I'm here for the lunar ceremony with a… conquest." He tilts his head towards me.

Playing along, like I did when we encountered the treeman, I adopt a simpering expression and ignore the pounding of my heart in my chest. *I am his deceived bride*, I try to mentally convey to the guards. *There's nothing to worry about*. But my body remembers pressing against him hours earlier, and the confusing feelings curl through me again.

The guards exchange glances, their silent communication almost a language of its own. For a minute, it seems like they might challenge us, but something in Silas' demeanor must convince them otherwise. With a grunt, they part, allowing us passage.

"You're cutting it close," one growls, one with a fish head. The words sound like they're being gurgled from underwater. "Full moon is in two days. You need to hurry."

I blink; the phrasing sounds nearly identical to ones Silas had barked at me during our journey. *Do selkies and finfolk deal with the full moon?* I consider werewolves. *They do, perhaps it's a shapeshifter thing.* But a niggling thought reminds me of his lie at the Island, about sirens.

"Move along then," another guard growls.

Silas nods in mock salute. "Come, girl," he says, reaching for my hand again. I hesitate, my eyes narrowing as questions continue forming.

"Silas, who—" I begin, but he cuts me off with a look.

"Later," he mouths.

I nod, remembering our audience and hoping they missed our byplay.

As we pass the guards, their eyes follow us, and I feel Silas' unease like a weight around my neck. We're too far in now, and I can't help but wonder if there's a way out—for either of us.

We slip under a waterfall that drapes like a curtain, opening into yet another giant cavern, this time with layers and tunnels like a rabbit's warren. The hollowed-out space is alive with bioluminescent faelights, clinging to corals and anemones that coat every inch of the walls, the only light sources. A wall of water forms the ceiling above us, illuminating schools of fish that appear to be flying and vibrant blue-green currents of the ocean. Every breath is tinged with seaweed and algae, reminding me that we are deep beneath the surface. It's beautiful but unnatural, with all the water sucked from the space and air pumped in. At the center of the cavern is something that looks like a palace made entirely of pearl, glimmering in the dim light. Humans scurry about, dressed in tan rags, their expressions a mix of fear and resignation as they go about their tasks under the watchful eyes of their finfolk captors. The atmosphere is heavy with an oppressive silence, broken only by the distant echoes of dripping water and the occasional murmurs of conversation.

Just as I open my mouth to suggest the next part of a plan, a harsh wave of laughter crashes over us. Behind us stands a figure that looks like a god of the sea, with sharp features carved from coral, rippling muscles, luscious black hair, and skin the color of sun-bleached sand. But there's a coldness in his swirling blue eyes that makes me want to baring my teeth.

"Silas!" he calls out, his tone dripping with mockery. "Didn't think you had it in you."

Silas tightens his grip on my hand and his fear radiates through our intertwined fingers, mirroring my own anxiety.

Who is this finborn? And... how does he know Silas?

I dart my eyes between the finborn and Silas, a storm brewing in my mind. I want answers, but the words won't come.

"Thought you'd never catch a human of your own," the finborn continues, stepping closer. His eyes are dark and menacing, like the ocean depths where light fears to tread. He claps Silas on the back, a gesture that seems both camaraderie and threat. "What with the stick up your tail about those fae-cursed laws."

Behind him stands another group of finfolk, their predatory gazes fixed on me with unsettling indifference. A sense of foreboding settles into my stomach.

"In fact," the finborn sneers, circling us like a predator sizing up prey, "I thought you wouldn't wake when we dumped you in the north."

The others watch with detached interest.

"Shows what you know, Jett," Silas replies tightly. My fingers slip from his grasp, and my gaze locks onto his in shock. "I found her there," he continues, "in that forsaken place and still followed the laws to the letter. She may not be fully human, but she counts enough for us."

His words are like daggers, each one piercing deeper into my heart. I look at him, searching for any sign that this is all a twisted joke, but his expression is inscrutable. Instead, he slowly changes before my eyes. His form shimmers and ripples like sunlight dancing on the surface of the water, his skin taking on a sheen that reflects the colors of the deep sea, the pale color turning dark blue. Gills form along his neck and a large fin bursts from his back, tearing the borrowed shirt he'd still been wearing. His face keeps the same features, no half-fish here, and so do his eyes—piercing and filled with an emotion I can't quite name. In a breathtaking transformation, he morphs into his true self: tall, majestic, and undeniably a finborn.

I should be horrified. I should be screaming in terror at the sight unfolding before me. But instead, an odd sense of calm washes over me. *Of course*. Of course this happens to me.

Jett's grin widens, revealing sharp teeth that glint in the dim light. "I must say, Silas, we're impressed." His words slither through the air like serpents, coiling around my fears. "She certainly looks human."

"She's never transformed," Silas says, speaking about me as if I were not even present. "Like a newborn."

"Never doubted you for a second," another chimes in.

"Nor should you," Silas replies.

With a sharp snap of his fingers, Jett commands, "We'll put her with the others."

Rough hands seize me. There's no time for questions, no moment for fear. The finfolk drag me away, and I'm powerless, drowning under the weight of his treachery.

"Don't hurt my human, you only get one first ritual." Silas' plea follows me down the hall, but I barely hear him. His figure recedes into the shadows, swallowed by the depths of this cursed place.

The grip of the finfolk remains unyielding as they pull me further away from Silas, and into the unknown ahead.

I steal a look over my captor's shoulder, catching glimpses of the labyrinthine passageways lined with luminescent algae and strange underwater flora. The colors and shapes blur together as we dash through the winding tunnels.

The group of finfolk split off once they realized I wasn't fighting them. Now, there isn't one of them at each limb, but a single finborn with a fish face. He hoisted me over his shoulder and carried me aloft.

Instead of attempting to flee while being carried off to Gods knew where, I try to make sense of the betrayal unfolding before me. Maybe this was all part of the ruse: being taken 'with the others' only to reunite with Mama and escape together, Silas leading the way out. But deep down, I know there is more to this situation than meets the eye.

Because... none of that explains how those finfolk knew him. The pieces come together in my mind, forming a picture I don't want to see. Silas was a finborn and had lied about his species.

Vivid memories flash through my mind: the way he guided me here, the moments of vulnerability he showed when discussing his past, all now tainted by his deception. He needed a human for some kind of lunar ceremony in two days, but couldn't break the 'rule' against human trading. The other finfolk don't care, but Silas is too rigid for that. *It isn't a moral issue*, he'd said. *Rules need to be followed*, he constantly claimed. That's why he chose me, thinking that I was not fully human.

The finborn carrying me grunts as we round a corner, entering a chamber filled with other captives ready to be taken to their cells. Women and men huddle together in fear and confusion. I scan their faces, searching for a familiar one, but my eyes won't focus, clouded by the anger and misery of betrayal.

Why does Silas think I'm not human?

Chapter 10

Selkies, on the other hand, have a strong attachment to their seal pelts, which are essential for their transformation between human and seal forms. While selkies may sometimes hide their pelts to prevent theft or unwanted attention, they often keep them within reach. Unlike finfolk, selkies do not exhibit any residual aquatic features after exiting the water; their appearance remains fully

> *human until they actively don*
> *their seal skin.*
>
>
> -Excerpt from Beneath the
> Surface: Unveiling the Myster-
> ies of Selkies and Finfolk.

The curiosity fades, once I see what's in store for me. As soon as we're all gathered in the chamber, a hulking finborn grunts and starts shoving us through different doors. My door opens into another maze of dark, damp corridors, the walls covered with moldy green seaweed that seems to writhe in the faint light. The stench of stagnant water, rotting algae, and mildew fills the air, choking and putrid.

"Move," the guard barks, shoving the woman in front of me forward. She stumbles and is kicked into a bare cell. The same fate awaits each captive as they are pushed and tossed into more cells.

With each step deeper into this stronghold, I sink further from hope. I try to keep my head held high and my gaze steady, but inside, fear and anger churn like a raging storm at sea. We pass countless cells, some overflowing with people while others sit empty. In each one, I search desperately for any sign of Mama—her hair, her swirling brown eyes—but all I find are strangers staring back at me with the same bleakness that now weighs heavy in my stomach.

Finally, he stops me in front of a door, its iron bars as cold and unforgiving as my fate. Inside is a cell barely bigger than a closet, with another shadow already curled up in the corner. My new roommate. The guard unlocks the door, and I stumble inside before he can unceremoniously shove me in.

"Get cozy," he sneers before locking the door behind me.

The darkness is near complete, except for the sliver of light from the hallway. It doesn't pierce the gloom so much as highlight it—emphasizing every corner where despair lurks. I scrape my hand over my eyes to stop the frustrated tears eager to fall.

Instead, I collapse onto the hard, damp floor, the cold seeping through my bones and settling deep within me. Anger boils beneath my skin, a fiery contrast to the icy dread that grips my heart and the frigid bite of this subterranean prison. Silas, that treacherous finborn, had led me here under false pretenses, promising to reunite me with Mama only to deliver me into this wretched abyss.

"Hey," whispers a voice from the other side of the cell. "You'll be alright."

I want to hold on to that voice, to believe it like a lifeline. But deep down, I know the bitter truth lodged in my throat: their version of 'alright' was not the kind I wanted. I'll be alright as a captive, I'll be alive. But I will never truly be 'alright' again in this cell.

"Who are you?" I ask.

"I'm Rhiannon," the voice replies, closer now and more melodic. I can just make out a faint outline of a young woman, her features hidden in the shadows. "And you're Maeve, right?"

Surprise jolts through me at the mention of my name. "How did you know?"

"I heard 'em talking," Rhiannon explains, her tone tinged with sympathy. "About the new girl someone named Silas brought from the surface. Said she was *unique*."

I can't help but let out a bitter laugh at that. *Because he thinks I'm not human.* "I'm not. I'm just me."

"Whatever you are, 'least I'm not alone anymore," she says. "Whoever took me is supposedly *important*," she continues, her voice an angry growl now. "I've been stuck in this cell solo since he snatched me."

"How long have you been here?" I ask her.

"Depends," Rhiannon replies. "Samhain just finished when I was taken. How long's it been?"

My mouth drops open in horror. She scoots closer to me, revealing a petite woman clad in rags with ruddy skin speckled with dirt and grime. Her short red hair sticks up in all directions like an angry pufferfish. But it's her defiant green eyes that capture my attention, despite the desperation in her posture.

"That long, I take it," she says, sounding more matter-of-fact than defeated.

My heart clenches at the thought of spending almost a year in this desolate place. Eleven months of darkness, of dampness, of uncertainty and fear gnawing at the edges of my sanity. My fingers trace the cold, rough stones of the cell, realizing that time here must be marked not by the sun's rise and fall, but by the slow erosion of hope.

"Samhain is only a few weeks away now," I tell her gently. "After the next full moon, the hunter's moon."

She purses her chapped lips, her eyes reflecting a mix of resignation and something else, acceptance, maybe. "So, it's time then. At least my wait is almost over."

"Almost over?" I echo. "What do you mean?"

"Wait 'til nightfall," she advises quietly. "That's when the guards switch shifts, they stop listening in on our conversations."

I nod, grateful for any small sliver of hope to cling onto. Anything to distract me from the suffocating fear and anger that threatens to consume me in this cell. I try to come up with something benign to discuss to bide the time. Nightfall can't be much longer now. We'd come through the portal at dusk here, with only an hour in the Avalaruin cavern to the finfolk settlement. I internally wince, remembering how I'd trusted Silas, how kind he'd been.

"You didn't know it had been that long imprisoned here," I finally say, more of a statement than a question. If she managed that long without noticing, maybe life as a captive won't seem so unending. *A few hundred years, you don't live that long*, Silas said. *Was he imagining how long I'd be stuck here?*

A solemn expression shadows Rhiannon's gaunt features. "Time's different here. It stretches and warps, playing tricks. Days bleed into nights, seasons merge. It's hard to keep track of how long I've been trapped in this watery prison."

"Where did you come from?" I ask, shifting to face her. "Aboveground, I assume?"

"Yes," she says, sounding wistful. "Just north of the vampire territory, a small village there."

"I was north and east of that. It must've been... different," I say, unsure how to address the reality of living so near to creatures most only knew through frightened whispers. Given she's been living with the physical manifestation of my childhood nightmares—the finfolk—for the past year, it probably wasn't so bad.

"Most folks there dream of being turned." She scoffs lightly. "Chasing immortality like it's some kind of prize. But not me. I just want to live, you know? Really live."

And now she's here. And now I'm here. So much for freedom.

"To live," I repeat. It's a simple yet profound wish, one that resonates deeply within me as well. I inch closer to her, our shoulders almost touching in the cramped space. "I understand," I murmur softly. "I just wanted to find my mother, to be with her again." The ache in my chest threatens to overwhelm me as the image of Mama's gentle smile dances at the edge of my thoughts.

Rhiannon's gaze softens, her eyes mirroring the pain that I'm sure reflects in mine. "All searching for something, aren't we? Sometimes... sometimes it feels like the harder we search, the further away our hopes slip from us."

"You haven't heard of her, have you?" I ask, trying to find an inkling of hope here. "Her name is Marta. She looks a lot like me, just thinner. She's got brown eyes like mine, brown hair, tan and freckled skin that—"

Rhiannon cuts me off. "Never overheard that name. Most of us don't get names. You because of your uniqueness—" she jabs me in the stomach, her elbow sharp and bony, "—but the rest of us are just cattle."

My heart sinks, but I nod in understanding. We settle into silence, and I count the minutes until nightfall.

Night finally swallows the prison, and with it comes a hush of secrets. The guards' steps grow less frequent, their shadows merging with the darkness that clings to every surface like a second skin. I crouch by the bars, straining to catch whispers from the cell across the narrow passage.

"Hey," a raspy voice cuts through the quiet, "you new?"

"Yes, who are you?" I ask, my tone low.

"Call me Jorin," he says, and there's a shuffle of movement as he leaned closer to the divide between us. I can barely see his face bisected by the bars. His skin is the same shade as the golden brown of my eyes, but his own are bright green.

"Nice to meet you," I say.

Rhiannon laughs, at my politeness or something else. "Jorin, Maeve says the hunter's moon is in two days."

"Damn," another voice in the dark exclaims. "I thought we had at least a week."

"Who wants another week of this?" says another gruffly. "We just need to get it over with."

Rhiannon ignores the others who begin bickering over whether more time or less is better. "Maeve here needs to know about what's coming."

The conversation stops and I can feel, rather than see, all eyes on me.

"Oh, honey," a voice from the cell across the hall from us says. The voice is deep but feminine. "Yours didn't brag about what he was going to do to you?"

The thought bursts through me: *Silas isn't mine. He was never mine.* 'Mine' wouldn't do this to me.

"Lucky girl," says the same voice from before, the one wanting more time.

"But she's going in blind," replies his counterpart. "That's terrible."

"Will someone tell me then?" I ask sharply.

Jorin leans forward against the bar. "The lunar ceremony. Once a year on the full moon... the hunter's moon... the adult finborn choose a human. You're either bound in marriage or shackled in servitude to them."

"They can marry dozens of us, but we don't have to bear their children," another voice says, offering me scant comfort.

"Why do it then?" I ask. "Versus making us slaves."

"Power. Both are shackles but one is more subjugating than the others."

"Finfolk," I spit out the word like a curse. My chest tightens; escape isn't just an option now—it's imperative.

"Exactly." Jorin's voice holds a grim edge.

"And they do it every year?" I press.

"Once you're twenty-five, yes. And with each Hunter's Moon after."

This must be the point of the 'ritual' Silas told me about. The one he wasn't 'morally opposed' to, but for the illegality of human trading. I remember the long walk to my cell, and how many humans I passed. Apparently he only cares about that, and only enough to convince himself that a 'unique' non-human substitute, whatever that means, is acceptable. I lean back, my mind whirling with the horror of it. Married off or enslaved—neither future could be mine. I won't allow it.

I scratch my fingers against the floor, feeling the sharp edges of the rock below me. I gather a handful of broken pieces and lift it to the wall, trying to see them against the scant bioluminescent light. I recognize them as rocks I read about in the village library... and even some that are identical to the flint in my shoe. My eyes shoot to the steel bars of our cell. Finfolk, *not* selkies, are fearful of fire. That explains the lack of anything wood burning in the stronghold. But to a determined person, all you need is a flint and steel.

"Listen," I say, turning to Rhiannon. "We need to get out. All of us."

"I'm all for it," she says, a glint in her eyes. "But it's a fool's errand. Not that I mind dying to avoid servitude, but that's a coffin few will leap into."

"Maybe," I concede. "They take humans every year, right? There must be hundreds of us against *not-that-many* of them. We overwhelm them with opposition."

"But they're all hidden away," Jorin counters, eyes wide in the gloom.

"Except," Rhiannon interjects, her voice carrying a glint of something that sounds like hope, "the day before the full moon. They parade us before the elders. That's when each of them picks spouse or slave. We're all corralled together beneath the chamber, with a few human guards."

"How'd you know that?" a voice asks.

"One of the human spouses told me when I arrived," Rhiannon says, shrugging her thin shoulders. "Was the first to be here for a few months, so they kept me with the others for a little while."

"Are we together before the ceremony too?" I ask, a plan forming.

She shrugs again. "Not as a whole group, but the ceremony's in batches. We're kept in holding areas near the chamber."

"Then we need to get the word out tomorrow and we'll attack from our holding areas at the same time. Overwhelm them and break out."

"Fight? With what?" Jorin asks, the disbelief in his voice palpable.

"Fire," I answer, a mean smile curving my lips. "We'll burn this place to the ground."

The silence that follows was heavy, fraught with the weight of our shared desperation. But beneath it all, a spark ignites—a spark that promises rebellion and retribution. We cobble together a plan, a scant, wretched thing, born of rage and violence.

"Tomorrow," I say, the word tasting of both dread and opportunity. "We begin tomorrow."

As the night falls and everyone else drifts into sleep, I stay awake, leaning against the cold stone wall of my cell, my flint and firestriker crushed tight in my hands, turning the skin of my knuckles white. The hope of tomorrow may lull them to sleep, but for me, it is the fear of our impending failure that keeps me conscious.

Which is why I'm the only one who notices when the cell door creaks open, a sliver of light cutting through the gloom. My heart races as I shove my contraband back into my shoe, expecting to see one of the finfolk who've been holding us captive. But instead, I am met with a sight that fills me with rage: Silas standing in the doorway, his ragged figure against the glowing light. He's still in his finborn form, blue as the midnight tide. He's also found a shirt that fits around his back fin.

Guilt hangs heavy on his features, visible in every line of his face. For a moment, it seems like he might crumble under its weight. My initial instinct is to scream at him, to unleash all the anger that has been brewing inside me since his betrayal, to close my hands around his throat and cover up those gills. But instead, I stay silent, letting the coldness in my gaze speak volumes.

Until the silence becomes unbearable and I can't hold back any longer. "Are you just going to stand there?" I spit out, my words dripping with venom. "Did you come here to gloat? Or maybe to see if your betrayal was worth it?"

He flinches, pain blooming over his expression. "Maeve, I'm terribly s—"

"Save it," I interrupt coldly, rising to meet him with newfound defiance burning within me. "Any apologies you might offer are as empty as this cell."

"I tried to warn you." Silas' whisper cuts through the shadows, a thin blade of remorse. "I couldn't get the... the words out. I tried to turn us around. I did try, Maeve."

Ghosts of sentences he started and didn't finish, memories of his half-heartedly suggestion that we go to the selkies, flood back. Moments when his eyes held hesitancy that I brushed aside, thinking them insignificant in the growth of our friendship and trust, not realizing they were his own doubts.

I scoff, crossing my arms despite the chill that clings to my skin. "You think that absolves you?"

Silas takes a tentative step closer, his hands raised in surrender. "I never wanted to hurt you."

"Then why did you?" The question hangs between us, heavy and accusing.

"I did what I thought was necessary," he begins, unable to meet my gaze and instead focusing on the floor. "As a finborn... we are bound by rules, traditions. It's expected of us."

"Expected to capture and steal humans, you mean," I snap, my voice dripping with scorn.

"Maeve, you must understand," he starts again, each word sounding more hollow than the last. "It's a requirement to stay in the community."

"And again," I say, stepping closer, forcing him to look at me, truly look at me. "You want to stay in a community that goes against what you apparently believe?" I clasp my hands, feigning understanding. "Oh, wait, you don't care if others break the law, so long as your hands are clean. Well, guess what: they aren't."

"I have never captured or stolen a human," Silas corrects me firmly, but even his own conviction is crumbling like dry sand.

"Semantics," I spit, circling him now, the power shifting, no matter that I'm the one in the cage. "Even if you actually believe I'm not human, which— laughable. Do you truly think that because you didn't physically capture a human, it makes it all okay?" I gesture to the cells, only a handful I can see. "You're not just a bystander in this system, Silas. You're an active participant. That makes you just as guilty for the wrongs that are being done."

His eyes flicker with conflict as he struggles against the invisible chains that bind him to this place and these actions. In his gaze, I see a tempest raging against a calm sea, a harsher version of my internal struggle before I finally mustered the courage to leave my father. But even though it's difficult, it doesn't excuse him from the choices he made while in this system of wrongs.

"You can dress it up however you like, but legal or not, you've stolen me. You're enslaving a person. A person." My voice has turned to steel as I speak. "The way I see it, the books were right. You are all vicious monsters."

He flinches, and I know I've struck true.

"I planned to marry you. We would belong here together," he says quietly, like it's an offer that should please me.

"Lucky me," I spit out bitterly. "Just what every woman wants, being taken to the altar in chains, one in a line of other captives."

"We're in this now, Maeve," he tries to rationalize. "We had our chance to turn back, but it's too late now that—"

"We both know how much effort you put into giving us that chance," I interrupt with biting sarcasm. "For days it was 'we must hurry, Maeve' and 'we can't take a break, Maeve.' 'The moon is coming, Maeve.' And only a few hours ago did you even suggest it!"

"Because things changed for me!" He nearly shouts it into the cell. We both quickly scan our surroundings, making sure no one has woken from the noise. Rhiannon, laying beside the bars behind us, maintains the steady breath of sleep.

"Things changed for me, Maeve," he repeats urgently. "I... I thought this was my only option. It was either do the ritual or face excommunication or death. And then... I started to care for you. Your offer felt... real. A real life we could have, together." He runs an azure hand through his white hair, looking pained.

I gesture sharply around the cell. "Well, congratulations on winning me over, Silas. You know how to show your feelings. I'd hate to see where you imprison someone you *don't* like."

His voice softens as he steps closer, looking down at me with red-rimmed eyes. "But the kiss—"

My stomach churns at the memory and I cut him off with a sharp wave of my arm. Anger coils tight in my chest, a sea serpent biding its time. "No. Don't remind me of that. Just answer me one question."

He moves in closer, crowding me against the wall as he looks down at me with desperate intensity. "Anything."

"For fae's sake, why do you think I'm not human?"

He lets out a sigh and leans back towards the door, defeated.

"You're not human," he says quietly. "You're a selkie, like your mother before you."

"Stop lying to me, Silas," I snarl, my voice on the edge of breaking. "You couldn't even answer that without lying. You're the worst kind of finfolk."

Desperation creeps into his features as he shakes his head. "I'm not lying and I won't betray you again." He reaches out to take my hands but his grip is too tight for me to break free. "Please believe me, Maeve. Everything will work out. I promise."

Finally, I wrench my hands free from his grasp, rubbing my skin against my skirt to remove his touch. "Don't touch me," I snap. "Leave, but remember this as you do: Amara said you were supposed to discover a truth. Well, congratulations, you just learned that you're a liar and a betrayer."

"It is your truth to learn, Maeve. And you just did," he murmurs. And he leaves, the cell door closing behind him as I dig my fingernails deep into the skin of my palms.

I'm so focused on his retreating form that I only then notice that Rhiannon's eyes are open, watching me.

"Lover's spat?" she asks.

I chuckle bitterly, shaking my head and forcing down memories of that faedamned kiss. "Not hardly."

"I dunno, sounded pretty emotional to me. Like a break up," she says.

"We only met a few days ago when he was imprisoned by my father," I explain, meeting Rhiannon's gaze head on. "Now he's caged me in return."

Rhiannon studies me for a moment. "Was that common? Your father capturing creatures?"

"No," I answer, casting my memory back. "Not that I recall. He always wanted to though, talking about the finfolk and those monsters of the sea." But it was always just talk until Silas came into the picture. The first of his kind that my father had managed to capture.

Rhiannon leans in closer, resting her dirty fist on her knee. The nails are nearly black from their time underground. "I assume you rejected your father's actions and immediately freed him the minute you could?"

A frown forms as I contemplate her question. "No," I admit reluctantly. "It wasn't until he promised to help me find my mother." A promise he ultimately failed to fulfill, unless I find her in this hellhole.

Her expression shifts, as if she's come to a realization of her own. "Complicated, isn't it? Love and duty, loyalty and betrayal," she muses. "Sometimes they're all tangled up in one messy knot that's impossible to unravel."

Echoes of Amara's words can be heard in the pronouncement. I turn away from her piercing gaze, unable to face her knowing look. "I don't know what you're talking about," I mutter.

Rhiannon chuckles softly. "Don't have to admit it to me, but don't deny it to yourself. Because denying it is like trying to hold on to water. The harder you grip, the more it slips through your fingers."

"He's kidnapped me and planning on enslaving me through marriage," I tell her, aghast.

"Right, right," she says, still smirking. "Want to run through the plan again?"

Chapter 11

Interestingly, both selkies and finfolk exhibit a distinctive feature in their human forms: swirling eyes. The irises of both species display a mesmerizing, shifting pattern reminiscent of a swirling vortex, akin to the fluid motion that captivates anyone who gazes into them. While eye color is, like humans, genetic and dependent on a number of factors, no finfolk or selkie—even those with some human blood—has fully stationary irises.

-Excerpt from Beneath the Surface: Unveiling the Mysteries of Selkies and Finfolk.

When morning comes, two finfolk guards grab us roughly by the arms and lead us out in groups of six. We trudge through dark, winding passageways until we reach a large bathing pool, fed by streams of water dripping from the ceiling and seeping up from the earth. With water above and below so close together, it's as though I'm enveloped in a bubble inside the water. And yet that is the *second* most fearsome thing I'm experiencing today.

After our early morning wash, we'll be presented before the finfolk elders, each finborn parading their captured humans to announce whether they will be a spouse or slave. The scant difference between the two is enough to make me vomit up the dried seaweed breakfast they tossed inside the bars of the cells this morning.

"Move along, humans," a guard barks. They push us with their webbed hands, indifferent to our stumbling feet. My own shoes I left in the cell after Rhiannon warned me of the early morning dip, my contraband hidden deep within.

We line up along the edge of the pool, shivering as one by one, we're forced to abandon our last shred of dignity and undress. The chill of the morning air bites at my bare skin, and I curl my toes over the cold stone rim of the pool. The water is a mirror, dark and unfathomable, waiting to swallow us whole.

The dream... I had to remember the dream, when the water seemed kind.

"Jump!" a finborn snarls behind me.

"Embrace it," the whisper of that dream voice coaxes, threading through the fear. Breathe in, breathe out. I close my eyes for a heartbeat, letting the memory wash over me.

And then, without another thought, I jump, like a sailor steering into a storm. The shock of cold envelops me, filling my ears with its silent song. Bubbles dance around me as I sink lower, eyes shut tight. The chill seeps into my thoughts, nudges them aside, and there it is—the dream again. But not like before. A vision takes hold of me, sharper and clearer than before.

I'm swimming, but it's effortless, like flying underwater. The sea cradles me, knows me. With every stroke, every splash, the dread ebbs away, replaced by a burgeoning curiosity.

What does it mean to embrace the water?

Could Silas have been right? Amara's cryptic words echo in my head—was this what she meant? Is this my truth that must be revealed? That my path is what lies beneath, under the water as a selkie?

Mama isn't here, she's not with the finfolk, I know this now. Is she a selkie, then? Dad kept something important in his trunk, her pelt perhaps. Which means she wasn't taken from me by a finfolk, she took *herself* away from me, choosing freedom.

That's what I'm doing here, that's what all the humans will do tomorrow.

Or... am I to embrace my fate here among the finfolk? The choosing ceremony looms, but somehow, submersed in these depths, it feels distant, like a storm seen from afar. Something that won't touch me.

What about Silas then? What piece of the puzzle was he missing, that he didn't know—or couldn't tell?

I push aside the thought. Silas' choices and problems are his own. I let the water enfold me.

Memories flash—my mother's songs, her longing stares at the crashing waves, the way her swirling eyes would trace the lines of my face with a watery smile. And the dream from the lake, full of shapeshifters, but it was a selkie that reached out to me. It was a selkie that spoke to me.

Use your fire. Use your teeth.

I'm trying, I tell the dream-like voice. *I'll burn them to the ground, but I have no teeth.*

And then my skin tingles, itching in a way that has me wanting to peel it off, to reveal something hidden beneath. As the need for air claws at my lungs, I kick upwards, breaking the surface. Reality rushes back, loud and bright. But the dream isn't gone; it clings to me like a second skin, demanding to be understood.

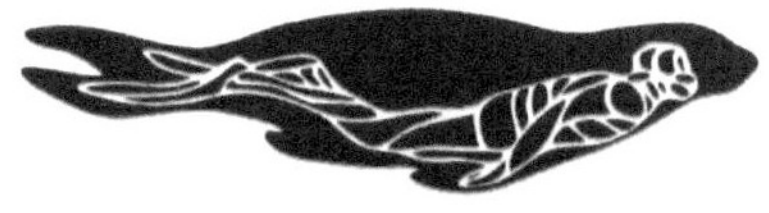

Forced together like fish in a net, we're taken to a tunnel beneath the pearly castle I'd seen yesterday. Unlike the beauty of the palace, this space is more like a tomb, an under chamber readying us for a dreaded fate. The walls are damp and covered in patches of dark mold, the floor littered with bits of seaweed and dead sea creatures. It's cold and smells like brine here, as if the ocean had crept in and left its mark.

When the finfolk leave to wait in the chamber with the elders, Rhiannon and I sidle up to the others we'd conspired with last night.

"All the humans have to walk in together with the captive they're stuck with." Rhiannon's voice is barely above a whisper as she explains what's to come. "When the finborn goes before the elders, every human they've taken will be behind them, trophies of their age and skill."

The hair on my arms stands on end at the explanation. Rhiannon gestures towards the other groups forming around us, creating a haunting display of servitude and domination.

"A few of us are best able to work the crowd," Rhiannon continues, "since our captors are only twenty-five this year. This is their first time taking part in the ceremony, so it's just us for now. Unlike some others..." She trails off as Joric is dragged away by an older woman and lost in a mass of what must be fifty humans. All 'belonging' to the same finborn.

Our plan is reckless, born out of desperation and a secret Silas accidentally let slip: their fear of fire. With my flint and firestriker, and the materials found in the stronghold, fire is our best chance at freedom. But our small group will be pulled apart in seconds, so we must act fast to let everyone know the plan.

"Spread the word," I say, locking eyes with each person, trying to instill confidence or maybe just borrow some of theirs. "We need flammable items to catch whatever the flint and steel lights. Anything you can find. Tomorrow, we're turning their entire world into an inferno."

"Are you certain this will work?" a woman from the neighboring cell murmurs, her voice laced with doubt.

I nod, infusing myself with self-assurance. "It has to."

"We'll show 'em strength. There are dozens more of us. And each captive is full of their own power," Rhiannon adds calmly, but I can see the fight in her eyes that matches my own determination.

"Groups of ten," she whispers to me as we split up and move between huddled bodies, our words quick and quiet. "Fast hands grab cloth, slow hands take the heavier stuff."

"Right," I mutter back, heart hammering against my ribcage.

"Listen up," I say, catching the gaze of a cluster of captives. After I explain the plan, I tell them, "You're group one. Gather tinder—fabric, paper, anything that'll light fast and you can hide under your clothes." They nod, eyes sharp with determination.

Rhiannon signals from across the way. Another group forms from the captives who have been here nearly all their lives, ones 'assigned' to the older finborn, a large band of humans with more freedoms but still trapped like us newcomers. "You," she murmurs, pointing to a burly man with scars crisscrossing his arms, "lead your group. Find oil, spirits, anything that burns long and hot."

We work like that, swift and silent, assigning roles. My pulse syncs with the urgency of our whispers.

The room shifts, an undercurrent of tension rising as the finfolk begin their procession. One enters, a brawny finborn with shimmering scales and white hair that's starting to gray.

"Out," he snarls. The first line of humans leave the room behind him like a twisted parade.

"Keep it hidden until tomorrow," I mouth to a woman whose hands shake as she tucks scraps of fabric into her sleeve. She nods back, lips pressed in a thin line.

I can feel it, the weight of every captive's stare, heavy with hope and fear. The finfolk don't notice, too caught up in their ceremony to see the storm brewing in our eyes.

"Remember," I whisper to a young man with a fire in his gaze, "it's about timing. Wait for my signal tomorrow. Even the smallest flame will incapacitate them."

"Got it," he replies, clenching his jaw.

But some eyes slide away from me, wary and afraid, while others hold mine with a blend of curiosity and hope. As whispers trail behind me like an eel, a shiver of unease that prickles my skin. I press on, feeling their gazes heavy on my back. It's not my plan they're unsure of; it's me.

"She's one of them," someone hisses.

"I'm not," I promise. "And even if I were, you should still listen to me. Find anything that can be kindling for the flames we plan to ignite."

Their fear of me doesn't matter, so long as they hear my words. Once I reach the opposite wall from where I started, I gather my own armfuls of flammable debris to shove down the pants I switched into before entering that blasted cavern from the forest. It's crude and uncomfortable, but it must be done.

A trembling hand grips my arm, and I turn to see one of the older prisoners, hunched and worn. "They fear you because they do not know you," he says softly, voice rough with years of captivity. His eyes pin me and it's like I'm looking into a mirror. The color within them swirls like a pool of honey.

"Your eyes," he croaks. "Child, they mark you as kin to the selkie."

Surprise punches through me, cold and sharp as the depths of the ocean, that he believed it, that it could be true.

"Impossible," I whisper, but even as I say it, the truth of his words settles into my bones. Silas I couldn't trust, but this man has no reason to lie. The itch from the morning returns and I want to claw off my skin, to reveal what's underneath. Reveal my... pelt?

A surge of conflicting emotions washes over me: anger at being kept in the dark, disbelief at the possibility of being a selkie, and a little wonder that maybe there's more to my story than I ever imagined.

"Believe what you will," the old man says, his gaze steady, "but it changes nothing. You have a plan?"

"Y-yes," I stutter, grappling with this shift in my world. I don't have time to consider the implications. "We burn the chamber. Tomorrow. Use slate that makes up the floors as flint and the steel from the furniture."

"Good." His nod is firm, resolute. "Then lead us, half-selkie. Show us the fire in your blood."

I swallow the turmoil, let it fuel my resolve. We will not be chattel. Human, selkie, whatever. Not tomorrow, not ever.

A finborn leads another large group from the chamber, one that Rhiannon has already spoken to, but they're coming faster and we're running out of time to get all the humans on our side.

Emboldened, I step into the center of the under chamber, eyes sweeping over haggard faces.

"Listen up," I call, my voice more steady than I feel. The chatter dims, wary eyes finding mine. I see fear, hope, defiance. It's time to harness that raw energy.

"For those who haven't heard already. Tomorrow, we end this," I declare. "We're going to burn this place down."

Murmurs ripple through the crowd, a mix of disbelief and curiosity.

"With what?" someone challenges from the back.

"Everything you can find," I say. "Cloth, wood, any scrap that'll catch flame. The floors are flint, the walls steel. They've left us with the tools for their own downfall." I hold their gazes, willing them to understand. "Finfolk are petrified of fire, they won't be able to stop us. We've got one shot at this. We'll be focusing our efforts on central locations. Rhiannon," here I gesture to her, "will explain more. But if you can't get to your assigned location, just light it up and run while they freeze in terror."

Skepticism hangs thick, but I push on. "We need to be quick, silent. Gather what you can, hide it till the time comes."

A woman steps forward, her eyes hard as the flint beneath our feet. Her jaw is set and her hands are clenched into fists. "And if we're caught?"

"Then we fight," I shoot back, letting the so-called fire in my blood surface. "There's more of us and we have nothing to lose."

Whispers swell into murmurs, murmurs into nods. I watch as doubt wavers, resolve taking root.

"Look," I press on, "I'm not asking you to trust me blindly. But trust in your desire to be free, to go home." My heart thunders, but I stand tall. "Together, we can do this."

The room holds its breath. Then, like the tide turning, heads begin to nod. Eyes that once looked through me now look to me.

"Alright," a gruff voice sounds from the back. "We're with you."

"Me too," another chimes in.

"Let's burn them down," calls a third.

My chest swells with their growing trust. We're united by the same fiery goal: freedom. And I'll be damned if we don't seize it.

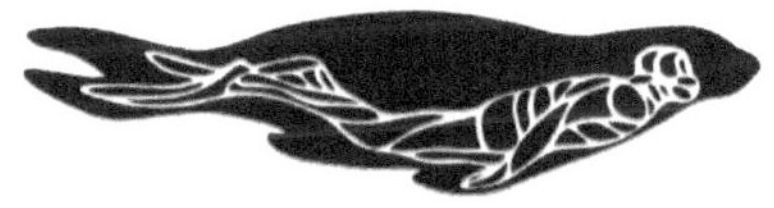

It's finally my turn, along with the other 'newcomers' who are experiencing this ceremony for the first time with their captors. Rhiannon is taken out of the room first by Jett, struggling against him. Her hands are forced behind her back in cold steel handcuffs and Jett drags her forcibly into the chamber, his laughter echoing off the walls like nails on slate.

Then Silas walks through the entrance, his eyes scanning over the small group of us left. His hair is tied back with two small braids around his head like a crown. Finally, his gaze settles on me and I can see a flicker of guilt before it's quickly replaced by a blank mask. A false smile plays on his lips as he gestures for me to follow him back through the door.

Heart pounding, I scan the chamber in the pearl palace—faces of humans and finfolk blend in a dizzying whirl of anticipation. The chamber itself is a dazzling display of shimmering pearls, reflecting the watery light that filters in from small windows high on the walls. The floor is smooth white marble, and intricate carvings of underwater creatures adorn the walls. I search for Rhiannon, needing to adjust our plan. Everything in this room is made from stone and pearl, which won't catch fire from my flint. But steel will, like her handcuffs. And we need more of it.

Silas tugs on my arm but I refuse to budge, planting my feet. He looks back at me with a pleading expression, one tinged with sadness.

"Maeve," he hisses. "You need to cooperate or they'll force me to handcuff you."

"Do it," I whisper back, baring my teeth. "Tomorrow, you'll need to put me in cuffs if you want me to take even one step."

He looks at me questioningly. "What are you planning?"

I remember the look he gave me yesterday, but I swallow it. "Nothing," I say, scowling. "I just don't plan on making this easy on you."

"I didn't expect you to," he whispers.

But his guilt doesn't move me. Not while we're in chains. Rhiannon is yanked forward by Jett. *Some of us are in literal chains.*

I let out a breath and allow him to pull me towards the platform that stands before a tall stage where a handful of finfolk elders sit. They hover above everyone else like sharks around a sinking ship.

"Next," one grumbles impatiently, and all eyes turn to us under the bright spotlight.

Silas hesitates for a split second, guilt flashing across his face before he buries it under his practiced mask of indifference. The crowd falls silent, waiting for his decision.

"This one," he starts, voice steady as a drumbeat, "will be my spouse."

The chamber echoes with murmurs, a wave of reactions crashing against the walls. I keep my face stone, but inside, a maelstrom rages. I think of my mother, and what I'd learned. Selkies are stolen to be spouses; it's as inevitable as lightning hitting the sea during a storm. I want to scream, offer a bitter laugh, anything. Anything to avoid the comparison now racing through my mind.

Rhiannon's gaze finds mine, a lifeline thrown across the chasm of bodies between us. Her eyebrows inch up, a silent question dancing in her eyes—the echo of last night's whispered doubts. Is Silas playing at love or simply my survival?

Either way, he'll surely burn with them.

Chapter 12

The most definitive way to distinguish between a selkie and a finfolk is to observe their transformation. Selkies will undergo a dramatic change when they slip into their seal skins, revealing their true nature as they shift from human to seal form. In contrast, finfolk display more subtle changes as they shift between human and full aquatic forms, retaining some of their humanoid fea-

> *tures rather than shedding an*
> *entirely different guise.*
>
>
> -Excerpt from Beneath the
> Surface: Unveiling the Myster-
> ies of Selkies and Finfolk.

Night comes and with it a sense of anticipation. Like the night before, I'm unable to sleep, my mind restless as I mentally trace the lines the bioluminescent coral casts on the cold stone floor of my cell. And, also like the night before, I have a midnight visitor.

Silas slips in from the cell. Idly, I wonder if he has the keys or if the finfolk don't believe we're a flight risk.

Surely someone *tried the door before.*

Silas' soft exhalation turns my attention back to him. "Maeve, I know you don't want to hear it," he begins, the words tumbling awkwardly from his lips like pebbles sinking to the ocean floor.

"How long did you know?" I interrupt. If he intends to disrupt my listless night, I'll at least control the conversation.

He licks his lips nervously, as if preparing himself for whatever reaction his words may elicit. "About?"

I raise a brow at him, unimpressed. "My being a selkie."

"Right," he says, shifting closer. He seems torn between sitting beside me or kneeling down, before finally choosing the latter. "I knew it after that first day, when you'd denied all I'd offered you. Your eyes blazed at me, and I knew you had to be a shapeshifter. Half-finfolk usually have sharper features so I took a guess."

I swallow a bitter laugh, trying not to wake Rhiannon, but it's likely she's listening. Even though my captivity is short, there's nothing to hide from a cellmate. "You guessed?" I scoff. "So you planned on bringing one of your *own* kind here and imprisoning them. Just when I think it can't get worse."

"No," he's quick to retort. "I only wanted to escape and the lie about finding your mother seemed like the best way to do it. I thought we would part ways quickly and I could convince the elders to let me stay without a human captive or simply start over somewhere else. But then..."

"What?"

He shifts uncomfortably, glancing around as though he doesn't want to look at me. "The night before, after our agreement but before you broke me out, I overheard your father and uncle talking. They were discussing finfolk and selkies... and how vile and treacherous they are, how they cannot be trusted."

I expect to feel dread, sadness, *something* at the revelation, but instead there's only a small sense of irony knowing that my own father doesn't trust *my* kind when he himself stole Mama from her home in the sea and created me. "Go on," I demand.

"And then," Silas hesitates, looking more nervous than ever, "your uncle mentioned something about how you always seemed to be drawn to the sea. He said you were too much like your mother in that way. And your father should be... exploiting that connection." His voice takes on a rather accurate imitation of Uncle Lorcan's hoarse tone. "What's the point of having a selkie kid if you can't use her to fish? Think of it, Gordon, we can sit back, let the seal bitch do all the work." He pauses, clearing his throat. "That wasn't me speaking about you in such a derogatory manner," he adds quickly. "I was simply repeating their words."

"No, I got that," I reply.

A heavy silence hangs between us as I process what he's said. I wonder how long Dad would have held out, before agreeing to Lorcan's plan and using me. I was already doing everything else, what stopped him? Did he have my pelt hidden away this whole time, something that had always been within reach but never touched?

Silas watches me carefully, his expression a mix of concern and guilt. "And that's what changed my mind about bringing you," he finally says. "You were already going to be a captive, so it wouldn't be worse if you came with me. And your being partly human meant I wasn't—" here he must swallow his discomfort because he looks pained, "—violating any laws and keeping myself 'clean.'"

More irony washes over me. The man who betrayed me may have ultimately saved me from a fate *worse* than imprisonment here. Despite his initial deceit, he's shown me a glimpse of the truth that would have remained hidden from me if not for his eavesdropping. But I won't thank him for the knowledge, not while those bars still hold me in.

"I did come here for a reason," he continues, undeterred by my silence.

"To release me?" I ask flatly.

Silas winces, as if my attitude is a physical blow. Slowly, he lifts his shirt to reveal taut, blue skin, and a parchment tucked halfway into his pants. He withdraws it, crinkled and worn at the edges, and holds it towards me. "Yes," he says quietly. "Or as best as I can do."

I snatch the parchment from his outstretched hand, my eyes scanning its contents with a mix of disbelief and suspicion.

"It's everything you need to know to escape—the guard rotations, hidden passages... even secret details about the lunar ceremony," he explains.

He's right. Detailed sketches, annotations, and intricately drawn maps fill the scant pages, each one depicting vital information about the stronghold. My fingers trace the lines, memorizing the guard rotations, trying to commit every secret passage to memory. We won't need as much chaos now, just enough to distract them and take the passages to freedom.

"You can use one of the passages the spouses and children are taken through, before the ceremony." He sounds like he's starting to ramble. "They aren't allowed in the stronghold, but they'll be secured in an underwater retreat, a mile away. I should have put those on the map, I can—"

"Why do this?" I demand, unable to reconcile this unexpected gesture with his previous actions.

He runs his fingers through his hair, dislodging the small braids from this morning.

"Because I don't want a captive wife," he admits with a hint of bitterness. "Because I owe you for getting me out of my cage. Because I *do* care for you." His voice is barely audible, thick with emotions that remain unspoken. "I found what I was missing, like Amara predicted."

"Your spine?" I suggest wryly, eyes still on the parchment.

He huffs a laugh, one that sounds wet with emotion rather than humor. I look up at him then to see a genuine smile on his face, one I thought I'd caught glimpses of during our brief journey together.

"Something like that," he says. "I hope you make it out."

He stands, brushing his hands on his pants. "Goodbye, Maeve," Silas said at last, his silhouette framed by the soft glow of bioluminescence on the walls. "Good luck."

I stare at the empty space he left behind, the maps burning a hole in my conscience. Despite the anger and hurt still fresh in my heart, there is a flicker of understanding that ignites within me. He may have betrayed me, but his actions now feel like a glimmer of redemption.

Rhiannon hops up from her feigned sleep, snatching the parchment from my hands. "Might just work even better," she declares, pointing to various areas on the map. "We focus the flames here and here, sneak out through here. Just need to use whatever steel we can find." A vicious smirk tugs at her lips. "Elders sit on thrones, did you get close enough to see if they're steel?"

"I think they're pearl," I answer distractedly, still looking at where the ghost of Silas stood just moments ago.

"Damn. Would've been poetic to destroy 'em with their own seats. I'll have cuffs. You?"

I nod. "Silas promised me handcuffs tomorrow." Although he might be surprised to see me. The first opening in the guard rotation is in the few minutes after we leave the cell and before we get into the under chamber we were crammed into this morning. He likely assumes I'll be escaping then.

She turns back to me with a sly look in her eye. "And what about this Silas? Will you let him burn with the rest?"

I pause, my mind swirling with conflicting emotions towards Silas. "Should I even be considering it? He put me in here."

But was I any better? Releasing him only when he bartered something I felt I couldn't refuse?

Rhiannon leans back against the cell. "Love and duty and betrayal and loyalty," she reminds me softly. "All tangled together."

The threads of fate are delicate things, easily tangled and broken, said Amara.

I chew on my lower lip, the taste of salt and iron mingling on my tongue. "He's still a liar and a betrayer," I mumble, more to myself than to Rhiannon.

She nods slowly, her eyes never leaving mine. "And you still bartered his freedom."

"So we're both terrible people," I say with a snort.

"Terrible *creatures*," she says, stretching out her legs. "Little miss selkie."

I sigh, a long exhale that seems to carry some of the tightness in my chest away with it. "No," I finally say, in answer to her question. "No one deserves to burn if there's a chance for redemption. I'm just not... ready to forgive him quite yet."

"That's fine." Rhiannon nudges me with her shoulder, a slight gesture loaded with unspoken support. "Forgive when you're ready. Save him 'cause it's right. Fight 'cause you have to. And don't look back."

Chapter 13

Both selkies and finfolk are characterized by their insular nature. Selkies, despite their occasional forays into the human world, generally prefer the solitude of their oceanic habitats and are deeply protective of their seal pelts. This protectiveness can make them wary of outsiders, leading to defensive reactions when their privacy or possessions are threatened. Similarly, finfolk maintain a dis-

> *tinct separation from the hu-*
> *man world, often viewing hu-*
> *man intrusion with suspicion or*
> *hostility. Their secluded under-*
> *water realms are guarded with*
> *a combination of violence and*
> *isolation, making them less in-*
> *clined to engage with or accom-*
> *modate non-finfolk visitors.*
>
> -Excerpt from Beneath the
> Surface: Unveiling the Myster-
> ies of Selkies and Finfolk.

As expected—from Rhiannon's story and notes on Silas' parchment—we're taken to the ceremony in stages a few hours before dusk. Those of us who are to be spouses wait in the under chamber we were in yesterday; those to be slaves wait in the tunnels, based on some rot about our different 'statuses.' The already bound humans, those who have been in captivity already, wait elsewhere, sup- posedly preparing a feast for the finfolk to celebrate the Hunter's Moon. But hopefully, they're preparing to fight back against our oppressors.

The stone floor feels like ice under my bare feet. Ironically, they took our shoes from us this morning but left us in the same clothes we arrived with, meaning my flint is shoved in my pants with the rest of my makeshift kindling. I hand a captive without handcuffs my firestriker; they can use it to start a fire later.

They'll be assigning us our tan uniforms after the ceremony.

My gaze flits from one shadowed face to another—there's a twist of a hand here, a subtle nod there. I can almost hear the flints whispering from their hidden pockets, itching to spark rebellion.

I shift, pressing my back against the damp wall. "Ready?" I mouth to the man opposite me. His eyes, hard as flint themselves, give nothing away, but his fingers twitch in affirmation. That's all the answer I need.

A guard calls out, voice grating like stone on stone. They're moving us, herding the first of us into the ceremony chamber. We shuffle forward, chains clinking and ragged breaths filling the air. I keep my head down, playing my part, hands on my cuffs with my flint secretly resting in my palm. I could crush it with the pressure of my grip.

Rhiannon appears at my side, her eyes meeting mine in a silent exchange. Her grip tightens on the extra cloth she has wrapped around her waist. I sneak a flint out of the remains of her pocket and pass it to her. It shifts against the cold steel of her handcuffs, ready for action.

As we enter the pearly chamber, the air shifts. It's thick with incense and anticipation, cloying and heavy on my tongue. They're waiting for us, the finborn, their eyes gleaming like knives in the dark. I spot Silas near the front, his expression stricken. I can tell the moment he sees me, because his skin pales to a soft cobalt. Rhiannon and I exchange a glance.

Three, two—

Screams pierce the clamor from outside, frantic and raw. "Oop, guess that's our cue," Rhiannon quips with a manic grin. "Late to our own rebellion."

"Better late than never," I shoot back, finding a grim smile of my own.

Fire blooms across the room as captive hands strike flint to torch, setting ablaze everything that can burn. The chamber becomes an inferno of panic, finfolk shouting, their sleek forms scrambling chaotically. Some lunge at us, others sprint for the exits, their snarling poise shattered by fear. The air crackles, thick with smoke and the acrid scent of burning cloth and debris. It's a maelstrom of fins and limbs.

The chamber erupts around us, humans breaking away like a river bursting its banks. Screams melt with the roar of flames as we fight for freedom. Heat lashes at my skin as I dodge a finfolk guard, his spear slicing the air where I'd been seconds before. Through the pandemonium, I see Rhiannon leading a group of humans towards an exit, her determination cutting through the tumult like a sharp blade.

"Run!" The word is both a plea and command, ripped from my throat. The stench of smoke fills my lungs, the inferno's crackle chasing us, spurring us on. We can't look back—not now, not ever. Ahead lay life; behind us, only ash and chains.

That's when I find him again—Silas. He stands as still as stone amidst the havoc of the chamber, all color drained from his face. I rush to his side, shoving past a finborn who claws at the air, his face twisted in terror or rage—I can't tell which.

"Silas, come on! We need to go!" I yell over the din, shoving him desperately with my shoulders, hoping my voice breaks through the fear clouding his mind.

His eyes lock on mine, wide and unseeing for a heartbeat before recognition flashes through them. He blinks rapidly, chest heaving, then gives a stiff nod.

"Keys," he says, voice rough against the riotous backdrop.

"What?"

"My family... we were cold smelters. I have keys." The words were nearly lost amidst the cacophony, but I catch them, and a puzzle piece clicks into place. No wonder he moved through the prison like a shadow. And it reminds me just how little I know him.

With trembling hands, he fishes out a ring of keys from a hidden pocket, cold metal glinting in the firelight. A swift twist and my wrists are free.

"Let's go! There are more to free," I shout to him over the racket, but there's no time for thanks or questions. Survival is our only priority now.

We plow through the chaos, Silas and I, a pair of rebels with keys to every shackle.

We leave the palace chamber behind and enter the sprawling stronghold of the finfolk. My human allies are not idle, fire rages throughout the underwater world. Some finfolk have overcome their fear and are attempting to extinguish the inferno with water from bathing pools and from above us. But not enough have conquered their fear, and the fire is overwhelming.

"Here!" I cry, thrusting the metal into locks, freeing wrists, guiding dazed humans toward hidden passages. Silas' hands are just as quick, his knowledge of the labyrinthine tunnels beneath our feet invaluable. We move in sync, an unspoken pact driving us as we release one captive after another.

"Through there, keep low," Silas instructs, pointing towards a narrow slit in the wall barely visible behind a tapestry of shadows. They nod, eyes wide but still somehow trusting, even with Silas still in his finborn guise, and disappear into the darkness that promised escape.

"Move!" someone yells, a voice I barely recognized as my own. We surge forward, a mass of desperation and determination. A woman stumbles, her cry piercing the tumult. I reach back, hauling her up without pausing. Our feet pound the stone floor, our breaths ragged symphony.

"Keep going!" I urge those around me. No one needs to be told twice.

A sudden crash echoes through the hall we've chosen, followed by a guttural shout. The finfolk are rallying, abandoning their futile attempts to extinguish the fire, instead seeking out the humans responsible for it. A group—too large to count amidst the smoke—advances on us, their scales shimmering with malice in the firelight. My pulse hammers against my throat.

"Go!" Silas bellows, stepping between me and the advancing danger. His stance is firm; the smelter's son suddenly a warrior before my eyes. The ring of keys he gave me jangles at my hip, reminding me of our task at hand.

"Silas—"

"Run, Maeve! Find your way out!" His voice cuts through my hesitation like steel. The crunch of bone echoes as he blocks a blow aimed for my head.

"Promise me you'll find me!" I shout, desperation leaking into my voice.

"Go!" he grunts, blocking another attack.

I turn then, feet pounding on the stone pathway, as the sound of Silas' fight grows distant. Every fiber in my body screams to go back, but the keys at my side is another promise—a promise to free those I could. As I run, panting heavily, I lead another few dozen humans through one of the secret passageways.

"Keep moving, Maeve," I murmur to myself, breath coming in sharp gasps.

Legs burning, lungs screaming, I think I might burst, but I push on until finally, finally we breach the mouth of the cave. The world outside is a shock of sharp sunlight and crisp, fresh air that claws at my throat with every heaving breath. It takes a moment for my eyes to adjust, to register the blur of faces as more than just a smear of freedom across my vision.

"Easy there, you're safe now," someone says, steadying me as I stumble forward.

Safe. The word echoes in my mind as I glance around and struggle to recognize the familiar jagged cliffs and Unseen Lake beyond. Just two days ago, I was brought into this very cave through one of those entrances. My fellow captives huddle together, their expressions mirroring the storm of relief and disbelief raging inside me. We were out.

"Here, let me help with those," I say, moving towards a group still shackled. One by one, hands are freed, wrists rubbed raw by the unforgiving cuffs.

As the last set of shackles click open, a chorus of cheers erupts. Some begin weeping openly, overcome by the realization that they are no longer bound by the chains of their captors. Euphoria swirls in the air, a heady mix of adrenaline and newfound freedom. Groups begin to form, as those who knew each other in the underground prison find comfort and camaraderie in their release. Each freed captive's eyes hold a glimmer of hope, a spark reignited from the darkness.

"Someone needs to tell the fae," I mutter, watching men and women fall together in relief. "So this doesn't happen to someone else."

"Would it even matter?" Jorin appears beside me. He has a bloody scratch on his neck, and burns on his clothes.

"It could," I say distractedly. "If we can find my bag—if it's still there—I should have something for that cut." I point him towards an area that looks familiar. "Over there maybe."

Jorin nods and turns to leave, but I snatch his wrist. "Go in groups," I say. He pats my hand.

"I've got it, Maeve," he says gently. "Would you believe I was a ranger in my village? I know how to handle this."

I nod, slumping down to the ground. And then I laugh. I laugh and laugh until it hurts, until tears stream down my face, until my voice is hoarse.

It seems like an eternity before Rhiannon emerges, her fiery hair matted and her face smeared with soot, followed by what looks to be the last of the captives. I leap to my feet and meet her at the mouth of the cave. She wraps her cuffed hands around my neck and shoulders in a tight hug. I return the embrace just as tightly.

"Can't believe that worked!" she says, voice raspy against my ear.

We untangle ourselves and I unhook her cuffs. She rubs her wrists.

"Good news or bad news first?" she asks, clearing her throat.

My heart thunders in my chest, my mouth opening to answer, but she continues without giving me a chance.

"Good news: I did a last run through and all the humans got out." A mixture of pride and guilt surges through me. I hadn't even thought about checking. But she's not finished yet. "*And* the elders figured out I was one of the humans in charge, meaning Jett got dragged away for punishment."

"And the bad news?"

Her gaze flickers away from mine, back towards the dark maw of the cave we escaped from. "They know about you too..." She pauses and then adds quietly, "They took your Silas."

The news hits like a physical blow. I lean against the rocky wall, the keys suddenly slippery in my grasp. Jett, well, I can write him off easy enough. But not Silas.

"You could just leave," Rhiannon says, slicing through the turmoil. "Run and find your ma, go to the selkies. Leave him to his fate."

Run? The thought tempts like a siren's call, but for no more than a second. I can't abandon Silas to whatever cruel fate awaits him. "Damn it," I breathe, the decision tearing at me even as it was made. "I'm going back for him."

"Atta girl!" Rhiannon cheers, giving me a playful punch on the shoulder. "Knew you had it in you. Just be quick about it."

The keys jingle, a reminder of promises yet to keep. And with one last look at the scattered remnants of our captivity, I turn back towards the darkness.

Chapter 14

Moreover, the inherent distrust and territoriality of both selkies and finfolk only underscore the importance of avoidance. Their interactions with each other, marked by rivalry and competition, create an environment where non-aquatic outsiders are often seen as intrusions. Attempting to bridge the gap between these enigmatic beings and the human world can lead to unintended conse-

quences, ranging from magical mishaps to cultural clashes. Therefore, the safest approach for those seeking to understand or engage with these creatures is to observe from a distance and respect their boundaries, ensuring that curiosity does not lead to conflict or danger.

-Excerpt from Beneath the Surface: Unveiling the Mysteries of Selkies and Finfolk.

Water sloshes into my shoes as I sneak through the entrance, rising and rising with every step. My firestriker and flint are back in my pockets, ready for the epilogue of the rebellion if needed. The sound of rushing water grows louder as I make my way through the narrow passages towards the finfolk domain, the mossy stone walls slick with moisture.

Finally, I race through the waterfall and arrive in the stronghold, the castle looming before me.

I press myself against the damp stone wall. My heart thuds to a panicked beat at the watery vision before me. Water leaks from the ceiling, like a bubble that's been popped. The place is half-flooded, smoke still lingering in the air from our earlier attempt to burn it down.

Guards patrol restlessly, tridents and spears at the ready, their iridescent scales shimmering in sporadic beams of light from the bioluminescent flora. Using the map etched into my mind's eye, I maneuver through the maze-like stronghold, searching for any signs of where they might be keeping Silas. I slip through an archway into the pearly castle, water swirling around me, and duck behind a column. Kneeling, the water is up to my chest and my heart threatens to burst through my ribs. *Just breathe, Maeve. You've got this. You're a selkie for fae's sake.*

A flicker of movement catches my eye—a guard passing by. I hold my breath, count to ten, then creep forward. Voices echo down the corridor, growing louder as I approach the underdoor to the ceremonial chamber inside the castle, still ajar. I creep closer, pressing my ear against the gap.

"Jett and Silas will replace the humans at the hunter's moon rise," an elder croaks, his voice like gravel. "Those most harmed by the fire will have first choice."

"We have much to do," another elder says. "Now that we must restart the ritual."

The first elder coughs. "We have no time to purify them in the pools. Bring them to the chamber in an hour's time.

I back away from the door, mind racing with this new information. No one knew, or could explain *why* the finfolk had their ritual the night of the Hunter's moon. But from what I've overheard, it's something they're planning on doing, human captives or not. Which means Silas is in even more danger than I had realized. A shiver runs down my spine. I have to move fast, or it'll be too late.

Water laps against my thighs as I inch back to the prison, clutching Silas' keys tightly in my hand. If the water keeps rising, there will be no dry tinder left for my firestriker and flint to spark a flame. Unlike in the central chamber, here the guards roam languidly, unaware or unconcerned about the recent rebellion that took place. A splash, rhythmic and soft, signals the changing of the guard, just as Silas' parchment predicted.

Now.

The word surges through me like an electric current. I dart forward, shadow to shadow, moving like a ghost through the murky depths.

A cell looms ahead, occupied by a lone figure silhouetted against the faint light coming through a barred window. I take a chance that it's not Jett inside and he won't raise an alarm.

With trembling fingers, I fit the key into the lock and turn it slowly. The clang of metal clicking against metal seems deafening in the stillness of the prison. My breath catches in my throat as I push open the door, wincing at the faint creak it emits.

"Silas," I whisper, barely audible above the sound of water lapping against stone. Our eyes meet and his quicksilver gaze swirls with surprise before recognition lights them up.

"Maeve," he whispers, relief flooding his features.

"We must leave immediately," I say. The water continues to rise ominously, swirling like a treacherous serpent.

Silas nods. "I trust you," he says simply, and a surge of warmth rises in my chest at his words. Together, we move through the flooded corridors, our footsteps splashing softly as we evade the patrols.

A splash behind us—too loud, too close. I spin on my heel, Silas mirrors my movement, our backs pressing together. The finfolk guards advance in a tight formation that speaks of countless drills. We both know we can't take them head on, but perhaps we can outsmart them.

We lunge, not at them, but past them, ducking low. Their reach casts wide, hoping to ensnare us, but we're already slipping through their webbed fingers like water through netting. Silas' hand finds mine, and we run, water churning around our waists like chains trying to drag us down.

"Stop them!" a guard roars, the sound bouncing off the dripping stone walls.

I pull Silas along, my free hand slicing through the water, feeling for obstacles, for hope. The stronghold's lament grows louder, the song of impending doom. These creatures may have feared fire, but they wield water without mercy.

"Keep moving," I pant, my strength waning against the relentless tide. The surface seems miles away, taunting us with its promise of air and freedom.

Then, the stronghold groans—a deep, ominous sound—and the water level surges. It's up to my chest now, cold and relentless.

More splashes echo behind us as we struggle to keep moving forward. We aren't clear yet. My pulse thunders in my ears, drowning out the fear as my legs pump harder. Silas starts swimming and I try to do the same, but panic sets in and I can't bring myself to fully submerge.

"Come on!" he urges, now pulling me forward, hand clasped tight around mine as his powerful legs try to propel us forward. But I'm nearly dead-weight.

Where is the dream now? Where is my so-called selkie affinity for water?

Years of ingrained terror are hard to overcome in just a few days, no matter how hard I try.

"I'm doing my best," I hiss back, my breath coming in quick gasps as the icy water rises inch by chilling inch.

"You're a selkie," he reminds me. "Swim, Maeve."

"I don't know—" Another wave, and the water hits my chin, stealing the rest of my sentence.

But the water is a hungry beast, rising with an insatiable appetite. It licks at my neck, my cheek, eager to claim me as its next meal. I flail in a futile attempt to keep my head above the water as another wave knocks me off my feet.

I claw at the air, struggling to swim and stay above the flood, trying to tap into my inner selkie. Silas turns towards me, reaching out with one hand to grab me, but before he can reach me another surge of water pulls him away. He fights against it, swimming back towards me, hand out-stretched—

Until he's suddenly yanked backward through the water like a plug being pulled from a drain. The finfolk guards, swift and agile underwater, have captured him in their iron grip. They disappear into the maze of tunnels within the stronghold.

"Silas!" I shout, the sound muffled by the encroaching deluge. It's nearly covering me now and I bob uselessly in the water, trying to force my legs through the resistance, my heart pounding against my ribs. The cold of the water seeps into my bones, but fear keeps me moving. It isn't just the water—I'm drowning in dread. They have him, and I'm losing time, losing air, losing hope.

I make it out of the prison tunnels, bursting out towards the center of the stronghold with the makeshift tide. But the water isn't finished rising yet and I gasp for air, my head barely staying above the surface as I'm slowly pulled towards what used to be the ceiling. Soon, the entire stronghold will be underwater—reverting to its natural state before they created this unnatural pocket of air. Through the haze, I see the guards dragging Silas and Jett into the pearl castle. The water's back at my chin again, every breath a desperate pant. My mind screams for oxygen, for a plan, for anything that could save us.

But I can't give up. I kick and push myself towards the castle in the center. The entrance is below, completely submerged now. I plunge into the under chamber, water enveloping me completely, silence swallowing any of my cries. Instinctively,

I paddle upward, my arms straining against the weight of the water that surrounds me. But there is no surface to break through in the under chamber, no escape from this watery expanse. The ceiling presses down on me like a whale's stomach, while below an endless expanse of darkness yawns open, threatening to swallow me whole.

"*Use your fire*," whispers the memory of a dream, "*use your teeth*."

But I have no fire left under water—no flame to wield, no heat to summon. And my teeth? What use were human teeth against the thick scales of the finfolk?

Pressure builds against my temples, the cold clasp of the sea a shackle I can't shake. Desperation claws at my chest, but beneath it, something stirs—a pulsing, primal force that whispers of salt and storm.

Somehow, through the darkness that clouds my vision, a vivid vision of the werewolf from the circus flashes in my thoughts—the creature with fierce eyes and moonlit fur. A shapeshifter, no matter what Silas said. He must shift at will, not bound by the cycle of the moon. If he could do that...

A flicker of desperate clarity ignites within me. I'm selkie-born, daughter of a shapeshifter. There is no pelt for me. There must be a way for me to transform, a secret thread of power woven into my very being. I just need to untangle it.

"Come on, Maeve," I urge myself, digging deep and trying to summon the wild magic of shifting that runs in my blood.

My lungs burn for air, my body aches for transformation. I will my blood to remember what it is supposed to be, my skin to recall the touch of the sea. For Silas, for freedom, for life itself—I had to become what I was born to be.

"Shift," I command the cells of my body, the marrow of my bones. "Shift now!"

A tremor ripples through me, racing like wildfire across my skin. *Use your fire.*

My body contorts, bones reshaping with the grind of earth's fury. The sensation is cataclysmic, yet as familiar as the tide, a memory ingrained in my core. My pelt—my birthright—erupts from within, cloaking me in its silken legacy. In the dark and submerged world, I become a sleek and powerful seal. My pelt shimmers like liquid gold, like my human eyes, with the freckles from my human skin dotting my form. And my short and thick human figure turns me into a muscular and sinewy predator.

I spare no time to bask in my success. Muscles surge with newfound potency, and I propel myself forward through the underchamber, cutting through the water with grace born of ancient rhythms, sweeping past where I'd waited with Rhiannon—with all the humans—only hours ago.

I burst into the now-underwater chamber, the ritual space inside the castle.

The elders float just above their pearly thrones. To the side, Jett sways in handcuffs, his hair a snarl around his head, his eyes promising death. Silas is contorted onto his knees, his body suspended by the water's currents. My eyes, now adapted to the aquatic gloom, lock onto the finfolk who hold Silas captive.

"Let him go," growls a voice inside my head, fierce as any tempest. My voice.

The elders and guards turn as one, all staring at me in my fury. Silas, suspended in the water, his face a mask of pain and defiance, meets my gaze through the swirling currents. His disbelief slowly turns into a flicker of hope. With renewed vigor, he strains against his restraints, a defiant gleam in his eyes.

The water bends to my will as I slice through it with unparalleled speed, heading straight for the finborn who dare to keep him captive. The guards recoil in shock at the sight of a selkie within their stronghold, while the elders' eyes widen in fear and disbelief.

They've never seen a selkie in full wrath. They've never seen me.

Use your teeth.

I lunge, teeth bared, aiming for the closest captor. The thrum of my heart matches the drumbeat of battle. My fins beat their spears and tridents away. Seal jaws snap shut on scaled flesh, the taste of brine and blood mingling in my mouth. With every bite, I tear at them, each wound a word in the story of our insurgency.

The stronghold quakes with chaos, water churning with my relentless attack and their attempted defense. The finborn are formidable, but they hadn't anticipated the ferocity of a selkie's wild heart, nor the crushing power of her teeth.

Silas seizes the moment, wrenching free from the loosened grip, pushing off toward freedom.

"Swim, Silas!" my thoughts urge him as I release the finborn in my jaws.

We surge upwards, muscles coiling and uncoiling with the ease of the ocean itself. Silas keeps pace with me, his strokes desperate and strong. My seal heart thumps wild with adrenaline, a drumbeat pushing us toward the light that beckons from above.

We break the surface, gasping, spluttering, the air a sharp slap against our wet faces. The moon is low in the sky, barely risen and a silent witness to our escape. Around us, human figures huddle on the rocky shore.

"Leave 'em be," shouts a voice. Rhiannon.

We swim to the shore, slipping out of the water and resting on the rock, dripping and triumphant. Silas falls to his knees and then heaves a heavy breath, nearly falling to his back. I sit above him, perched to haul him up with my teeth, if I must. But he catches his breath, reaching out, his hand trembling as it brushes my slick fur. His touch is gentle, a contrast to the chaos we've left beneath the waves. I nuzzle into his palm, wordless.

And then I feel it—change rippling across my skin, a shiver of fur to flesh. My pelt pulls inward, an embrace that's both a farewell and a reclaiming.

"Look," someone breathes, and I know they're watching me. Limbs stretching, fingers flexing—human once more. The seal slips away, a secret tucked beneath my skin.

"Wow," Silas murmurs, and I can't help but laugh—a sound that somehow feels foreign after the barks and bellows of my other self.

"Let's get you warmed up," Silas says, offering his hand. I take it, feeling the roughness of his finfolk skin against mine, the pulse of victory shared. Together, we walk toward Rhiannon and the others, our escape a story already turning into legend.

Chapter 15

My ink-stained fingers fumble with the clasp of my leather-bound notebook, a gift from Silas when we first arrived at this mystical village on the outskirts of the mage settlement. We settled here once things calmed down with the finfolk because of its proximity to Prism Lake and the selkies, although I haven't had the courage to visit just yet.

We used two of my shiny coins purloined from Dad's trunk to rent a small room overlooking the Lake. I'd asked Silas if he was concerned about benefiting from the stolen gold, but he'd just squeezed my shoulder and asked for a coin to purchase us supplies. He returned with new clothes for both of us, some provisions, a used copy of *Be-*

neath the Surface: Unveiling the Mysteries of Selkies and Finfolk, and two notebooks to write our own stories.

I stare out the glass-paned window, watching the beauty of the Lake before me. In the distance, a dark figure breaks through the surface, soaring gracefully through the air before submerging once again into the depths below. Pen in hand, I begin to write anew,

> *While Selkie children transform and retain a separate seal pelt, like adult selkies, as the authors in* Unveiling the Mysteries *correctly write, their book ignores a subset of selkie species: half-humans, the children of those selkies who are willingly or unwillingly joined with a human spouse—*

The creaky wooden door opens, cutting off further thought.

"Rhiannon sent a letter through the portal," Silas announces from behind me.

I turn to see him holding a letter in one hand and a bouquet of daisies in the other. The darkness of the hall makes him nearly glow in contrast, a splotch of glitter and brightness.

He's back in his human form now, his skin pale but still bearing traces of scales from our recent underwater excursions as I adjusted to shifting between my selkie and human forms.

Closing my notebook, I ask, "Did she say anything new?"

Rhiannon remained on the Avalaruin side of the realm with a few other humans, a contingent acting as makeshift ambassadors to the fae. They refused to return to their homes until it was certain that the finfolk would no longer abduct humans ever again.

Silas sets the daisies in a glass of water on our shared dresser before sitting next to me on the creaky bed, handing over the letter. "The fae elders are now formally aware of the treaty breach, rather than informally, whatever that means. But she seems pleased."

I scan Rhiannon's loopy handwriting, her excitement clear in the way the ink bleeds into the parchment in some spots. "You missed this part. They're planning a four-party aquatic tribunal. Representatives from the fae, sirens, humans, and selkies will gather to discuss reparations for the abducted humans taken by the finfolk."

Silas sighs, clenching his fists. I know he feels responsible for his kind's involvement in these crimes, for his involvement. But hopefully time will heal those wounds.

I fold the letter and tuck it inside my notebook, next to my unfinished chapter about half-selkies. "It will be an excellent addition to your chapter on why finborn steal—or stole—humans."

Because not only does the world need to know more about selkies, finfolk need to be less mysterious. Forewarned is forewarned, or so the books say.

I gaze down at my own partially filled notebook. "Hopefully I can finish my chapter today," I say, almost to myself.

"We can finish both tonight," Silas promises. "We have plans now, remember? To go to the selkie settlement."

"Right, the settlement." We've been putting it off for weeks. He'd suggested we settle here because of its proximity, so he could keep his promise to me. Promises to find my mother, to seek the truth, to confront my past. But hesitation continues to wash over me like the changing tides and we haven't yet gone.

I nod slowly, feeling torn between the desire to reunite with my mother and the fear of what that reunion might bring, now that I know the truth. "I don't know if I'm ready," I admit, my voice barely a whisper.

Silas studies me with his quicksilver gaze, eyes flickering over my face as if trying to discern my thoughts, diving into the depths of my soul. "We can go tomorrow," he suggests softly. "You don't have to do anything you're not ready for."

"The facts will be the same tomorrow," I explain. "She wasn't taken from me, she left me. How do I... reconcile that?"

"Your mother..." He pauses, searching for the right words. "Your mother had a life beyond being a parent. Just like you have a life beyond being your father's daughter," he says earnestly. "You don't owe anyone forgiveness. Not your mother, not even yourself. You have the right to feel anger, hurt, confusion. It's all part of your journey to find your true self."

You carry the weight of a thousand unspoken words, said Amara.

Love and loyalty and duty and betrayal all tangled together, said Rhiannon.

With a deep breath, I stand up, the worn wooden floorboards groaning under my weight. "Shall we go, then?" I ask, keeping my voice steady despite the turmoil inside me.

Silas' hand finds mine—he reaches for me without hesitation now—his touch grounding me in this moment of uncertainty. He kisses me softly, a brush of lips against skin. "We're together in this, Maeve."

We step out into the crisp autumn air, the leaves above us turning shades of amber and crimson. Colorful houses line the cobblestone streets, their windows reflecting the sparkle of Prism Lake in the distance. The settlement isn't far, hidden within the cradle of a rocky enclave along the edge of the Lake where the selkies make their home.

Silas walks beside me, his presence a steady anchor in the storm of emotions swirling within me. The scent of salt and seaweed grows stronger as we near the selkie settlement, a mingling of fish and brine that clings to the damp air. It's the perfume of my childhood and I nearly turn back in a panic. But I don't.

Don't look back.

The settlement comes into view, its small structures blending seamlessly with the natural beauty of the lakeside surroundings. Driftwood huts covered with sea glass sprawl before us, their roofs adorned with vibrant seaweed and delicate pearls. Selkies move about in both human and seal form, their movements fluid and graceful as they go about their daily lives.

My eyes scan the crowd. Faces, so many faces, all a blur of features that aren't hers. I search, frantic for that familiar set of eyes, that curve of smile worn by time but never forgotten. *It's been twenty years, will she look the same?* My heart pounds in my chest. *What does she even look like as a selkie?*

And then, amidst the ebb and flow of strangers, I see her. A woman with long, flowing hair the color of pitch, her eyes the same shade of swirling brown as mine.

"Mama?" The word barely a whisper from me, tasting of hope and oceans deep.

Her hands still, the cloth she's holding fluttering to the ground, a white flag surrendering to the moment. Time seems to still around us as our gazes lock. Disbelief flares wide in her eyes, sparking into joy, radiant as the first dawn.

"Silas," I gasp, his name a lifeline as I tug him forward, my pulse hammering louder than the surf against the shore. We surge through the crowd, every step lightened by urgency, by need.

Silas squeezes my hand gently, his touch anchoring me to reality. "You've got it, Maeve."

"Mama!" Now a shout, a call across the years that stretched thin between us.

She moves towards us, arms opening like the horizon embraces the sea, and the distance crumbles. We collide, a tangle of limbs, the warmth of her engulfing me. A laugh bubbles up, spilling over like a wave cresting in the sun.

"I never thought I'd see you again," she breathes, her voice thick with tears unshed.

"Me either," I say. My world, once fractured, knitting together in the hold of her arms. But I keep a tight hold on Silas' hand, his presence a steady hum at my back. There's plenty to discuss, plenty to still uncover, but this chapter will close, my heart beating a new story for myself into life.

Further reading

If you're interested in more of my writing, check out my website (**kmalady.com**). You can find information about my other projects, like *The Ascend Trials* (a romantic YA portal fantasy all about subverting tropes), *Threads of Fate* (an NA romantic fantasy series adapted from greek myths), and more!

You'll also find a bonus chapter in Silas' point of view describing his thoughts after a few key scenes.

And if you're looking to spend more time in the trope-ics, check out the below:

SHE WHO BINDS THE FAE PRINCE
A spicy romantasy novella

SHE WHO TURNS THE VAMPIRE
A sweet epistolary romantasy novella

SHE WHO CLAIMS THE ALPHA
A (sweet & spicy) interactive romantasy novella

AND MORE!